I0732148

LUANN K. EDWARDS

Only a Glimpse

Love Comes Again Book 1

LuAnn K. Edwards

Dedication

This book is dedicated to the real Keedryn.
Your generosity inspired me to name my main
character after you.
And to my family.
I am grateful for each one of you.

"For I know the plans I have for you," declares the
LORD,
*"plans to prosper you and not to harm you, plans to
give you hope and a future."*
Jeremiah 29:11

One

Mid-September
Nashville, Tennessee

My boss, Blake Conner, flung open his office door a few minutes before 1:30 p.m. and stormed toward me with a scowl on his face. I peeked behind me and back at him. He planted his hands on the edge of my desk. I stood and braced myself for one of his daily onslaughts.

"These minutes are inadequate."

I flinched at the sternness of his voice.

He straightened and slid a sheet of paper toward me. "You attended the meeting. Didn't you? Incorporate these edits and get them correct this time." He plopped the remaining pages onto my desk. "They must go out soon. I don't appreciate your making me appear incompetent. You should know that by now."

I glanced toward our suite door when Chad Warren, our president, entered. To my relief, he frowned at my boss and not me. Chad stared at Mr. Conner and nodded toward Conner's office.

The two men hurried inside and shut the door. I stood at my desk with my mouth open. What was his problem? I couldn't have messed up that much. As an administrative professional, I'd taken thorough notes for twenty years. I knew how to take minutes. But I hated to think I caused my manager trouble with our president. Would Conner be fired like the VP in Legal last week? I put my hand on my chest. Or were they discussing my termination since I seemed to bring my boss so much anxiety? I knew he'd try to convince Chad that I was incompetent.

This was the second time that day Mr. Conner humiliated me. The first happened at the meeting with the executive team that morning.

As the executive vice president, Mr. Conner leads these meetings. He stared at me, narrowed his eyes, and used a gruff tone. "I need the minutes finalized by 2:00 p.m. and no later."

I'd never heard him talk meanly to anyone else. Only me. Grumpily? Yes. Meanly? No. I'd been his executive assistant for three months, and I attended these meetings often and never missed his 2:00 deadline.

Bottom line—he wanted me gone. Soon. *He should do us both a favor and transfer me out of here. I only hope he doesn't fire me.*

Chad's a likable man. Friendly and kind. Balding with white hair above his ears. He could easily add a beard and play Santa. His office is in the executive suite across the hall, and Beth Davis, one of my good friends at work, is his executive assistant. *Lord, if I'm going to be let go, I'd rather Chad tell me than Mr. Conner.*

After several minutes, Chad stepped into the front office where I sat reviewing the minutes and closed Mr. Conner's door. "I need to attend a meeting, but I'd like to talk with you. I'll stop by later today or tomorrow." He strode out into the hallway.

Was he upset? He seemed calm. I hoped we could talk later that day. I knew I wouldn't be able to sleep that night without knowing if I could keep my job or not.

The minutes would not be late. The edits were minor. They weren't even worth mentioning. But he was the boss, so I focused on meeting his deadline.

I looked up when Tauni Fisher, an administrative assistant from our Insurance Department, sashayed through the opened door and into our suite. Tauni, a young woman around thirty, radiated confidence and beauty—two things I lacked.

She seated herself across from my desk without an invitation. "I'd like a couple of minutes of your time."

"I'm rather busy just now." I tried to sound perky. "May I stop by your desk in about fifteen minutes?"

"That won't be convenient for me." She spoke in a snobbish tone. "I heard you received your promotion because Blake requested you."

I didn't have time for this. Not with Mr. Conner ready to pounce and rip me to shreds.

"I'm sorry." I shrugged. "I'm on a deadline. We can discuss this later."

"No, we can't. Are the two of you dating?" She pulled her long blonde hair behind her ear. "That's what I heard, anyway."

"Each other?" I jerked my head back. "You want to know if Mr. Conner and I are dating each other?"

"That's what I asked."

I didn't care for her snarky attitude and came back with a little sass of my own. "As of today, we're not dating."

"As of today?"

"And if we do, you won't hear it from me." I settled

back in my chair and clasped my hands on the edge of my desk. "Anything is possible unless he's already in a relationship."

Tauni rose, bent over my desk, and got in my face. "You know good and well he's available. You transferred up here to get yourself a husband. Everyone knows what you're up to, and I'll make sure it doesn't happen." She stood, walked over to Mr. Conner's door, and raised her fist to knock.

"Tauni. No." I jumped up and took a few steps around my desk. "I need to call him to find out if he's available to see you."

Mr. Conner opened his door. "Tauni, what brings you my way?" He motioned her into his office to the chair in front of his desk.

I placed my hands on my hips. I couldn't worry about her. Not with the minutes demanding my attention. I sat and got busy.

A few minutes later, when Tauni stepped out of Mr. Conner's office, he called out to her. "Thank you. I appreciate the information. And please close my door."

She sneered at me. "You can't have him." She traipsed off, grumbling to herself.

Is she out of her mind? Me with Blake Conner? My boss?

That woman got on my nerves. If she wanted him, she could have him. The two of them would make a striking couple.

I jumped at the blare of my desk phone's ring. Mr. Conner.

"Yes, sir."

"Are you finished yet?"

"Five more minutes."

He hung up without a word, and I returned to my task.

I didn't think I could take much more of this. How long should I stay in a job where I was unappreciated?

I sensed the Lord's tug on my heart. "He's hurting and without hope. Help him find peace and joy in Me."

Are You sure? Is this about his wife's death five years ago or something else?

And how could I share God's love with someone I didn't want to be in the same room with?

I hoped Mr. Conner and I could work this out. My late husband's medical bills drained our savings and much of his retirement account. I needed this job in order to save all I could to recoup our financial loss. I bowed my head and said a quick prayer.

I made the last edit and hit print to give Mr. Conner a copy for his final review.

His door opened, and he called out to me. "When will the minutes be ready? I needed those ten minutes ago."

I glanced at my watch. It said 1:55.

Everything in me, even after I prayed, wanted to run over to the printer, grab the minutes, and throw them in his face. My frustration level had maxed out for the day.

However, when I glanced at him, the Lord reminded me of His request and how Mr. Conner endured heartbreak and no longer had hope. I zipped to the printer, which sat outside his office door along the wall to his left. I smiled and handed him the minutes. "If you find anything else in need of correction, please let me know. I'd like to complete them to your satisfaction, Mr. Conner."

"Thank you." He reviewed the copy. "These are

fine." Without looking up he said, "Get me a cup of coffee. Black."

He'd never asked for coffee before. In fact, this was the first time anyone had requested that I get them coffee since I started at Boden Combs Healthcare more than two years ago. This would be an easy opportunity to get on his good side. I couldn't mess up coffee.

I hustled the short distance between our office suite and the employee break room. I found an empty pot. Great. This would take longer than I'd expected. I wanted to please him with at least one of his requests.

I stretched as far as I could to see on the top shelf of the cabinet.

"What are you trying to find up there?"

I turned. Wes Thomas, a coworker from Information Technologies, my former department, walked in.

"Filters. Mr. Conner needs coffee."

"I'll look for you."

I moved out of his way.

Wes must have been at least fifty but didn't have gray hair. Instead, he had short, dark brown hair and a mustache. He stood an inch or two taller than me, probably around five feet, six inches, and I hoped that would be enough to see the top shelf.

"Nope. None up here."

"Why are you here?" I tilted my head. "Don't you use the third-floor breakroom?"

"We're out of spoons. I figured the fourth floor would have everything since all the big-wigs are up here."

I shook my head and frowned. "Everything but filters."

I rummaged through the cabinets below the counter.

"They must be here somewhere. Wait, I found them." I pulled out a handful and placed them next to the coffee maker. "They were all the way in the back."

"Great. I know Conner. If he wants coffee, he expected it yesterday. How do you like working for 'The General'?"

"He's not that bad." I tried to hide my fib. Conner was brutal—hateful, heartless, and handsome. I exhaled and focused on the coffee maker.

"I'm not used to this machine. How does it work?" I opened the coffee container. "Does it take four scoops, like most coffee makers?"

"Executive Assistant Keedryn Reynolds doesn't know how to make coffee?" Wes chuckled. "Didn't you tell me you've been in the business for twenty years?"

I raised my eyebrows. "I'm not familiar with these fancy machines." I turned toward him and crossed my arms.

"No need to get offended." Wes picked up the scoop and showed me what to do.

"This will take too long." I moved the pot off the burner and held a cup under the spout.

Wes inched closer to me. "What about lunch tomorrow?" His tone was soft.

I twisted to look him in the eye. "I've told you before, I don't date men I work with."

"Lunch. Not a date." He grabbed a paper towel and wiped coffee grounds off the counter. "You have to eat."

"Thanks again for your help." I turned to the coffee cup.

"Let me know when you change your mind. We can talk about safe subjects, like the weather or business. Won't be classified as a date."

I looked up and watched him walk out the door.

Wes was a sweet guy, but I wished he would stop asking me to lunch. Sam and I were married for almost twenty-four years, and he'd been gone for three. There was no way I could find another man to take his place. He was one of a kind. The thought of dating after twenty-seven years terrified me. *Not going to happen.*

I left the employee break room and glanced at my watch. It said 2:08. I'd been gone for ten minutes. Conner would be upset and I'm sure would give me a lecture. Probably not something he did with his former assistant, Debra Arnold. He talked about her often. Meanwhile, I seemed to do everything wrong. Maybe he could get her to come back. What I thought would be an opportunity for advancement had become a nightmare.

I carried the coffee into his office. Relieved he wasn't at his desk, I took a step closer and noticed an available spot for the cup next to his mail.

"About time," he said from behind me causing me to flinch. "Did you have to walk to Starbucks?"

I spilled coffee on the carpet and his shoes. I raised my eyes.

He peered down on me. "I'm late for a meeting. Clean up this mess."

"Wait. Let me dry off your shoes before you leave." I set the cup down, grabbed tissues from his desk, and got on my hands and knees to wipe the coffee from his shoes.

When I finished, he left without saying a word. I plopped myself onto my backside and sat for a moment. I'd made a mess, and I was a mess. I knew my boss thought so.

I cleaned the spill from the reddish-brown carpet

and noticed how the flooring complemented Mr. Conner's deep mahogany desk, round conference table, and bookcases.

When I stood, I focused on the three paintings on his walls. One painting hung on each side of his conference table to the left of his doorway and one near his desk on the right. The painting closest to the table included cattle grazing in a plush green pasture with a small meandering stream. Reminded me of my childhood.

The second one was a romantic beach at sunset with water birds wading along the shore. I chuckled. If Conner were there, he'd yell at the birds for blocking his view.

The third painting hung to the right of his desk—a crystal vase filled with beautiful roses of various colors. I wanted to get a closer peek but was afraid Mr. Conner might come back at any moment.

I turned to leave and noticed a card opened on his desk. My curiosity got the best of me. "Happy Birthday, Allison. I love you to the moon and back. Dad." That was sweet.

I returned to my desk and remembered I'd never seen any personal photos of his family. Nothing on his desk or walls. Odd. Why no pictures?

I picked up a family photo of my daughter, Jenny Monroe, her husband, Carl, my five-year-old granddaughter, Nicki, and their beagle named Lucy. I adored my family. I set the picture down next to one of my favorites—one of Sam holding a two-and-a-half-year-old Nicki in his lap weeks before his heart failed. He left me too soon. I needed him to hold me and reassure me I was strong enough to deal with my boss.

I placed the photo on my desk and thought about my

work relationship with Mr. Conner. I'd done my best to be a great assistant, but nothing pleased him. I shook my head. I had bowed before him and polished his shoes. How humiliating. My shoulders sagged. I wanted to go home and relax with a good book and a hot cup of tea, but it was too early. I needed to pull myself together so I could face the rest of my day.

Mr. Conner whizzed past my desk a few minutes later and ignored me. I chuckled at the thought of Tauni's accusation. What a joke. Mr. Conner may be good looking, but I could never date him. As for Tauni, he's far too old. There must have been at least twenty years between them.

I paused with my fingers on the keyboard and thought about the first time I saw him—my second day on the job, and I was late. He stood near the elevator with a notepad in his hand and watched me make my way through the lobby reception area toward him. His wavy salt-and-pepper gray hair, dimpled chin, and the prettiest blue eyes I'd ever seen took my breath away. I didn't know who he was. I grinned. "Good morning."

He ignored me. He didn't even smile. He got into the elevator, blocked me from entering, and let the door shut in my face as though I were invisible.

I thought he must have been having a bad morning, but during the past three months I'd worked for him, it seemed every day was a bad day for Mr. Conner.

My computer pinged with a Skype message from "The General" that read, "Now."

My heart raced. What did I do this time? I bolted through his door.

"Take this to Marketing."

Relieved, I took an envelope from his outstretched

hand and turned to leave.

"Keedryn, my name is Blake."

I paused just inside his door.

"You may call me that if you'd like."

"Yes, sir, I will," I didn't glance back. After three months, I could drop the formality and call him by his first name. That, along with him thanking me earlier, was progress.

My next hurdle to cross—to see him smile.

Maybe there's a soft Blake under the hard Mr. Conner after all.

Two

Alone and exhausted at home in my recliner, I drank a cup of tea, put my feet up, and opened a cozy mystery that I'd started to read the night before. But I couldn't concentrate on the words. I glanced around me, thankful for my home. I lived in a building that housed four condo flats. Mine was on the ground level with a small front porch. My living room, dining room, and kitchen combination supplied me with enough open space to entertain a few guests—usually Jenny and her family. The hall to the right held three bedrooms. I converted the first bedroom into a TV room.

I had everything I needed, except for Sam. I missed him. He was a wonderful husband and dad. He put the Lord first and then his family. He inspired people with his charismatic personality and loved to tell stories about when he grew up on a farm. Jenny and Nicki adored him. With him gone, silence permeated the condo, and I was lonely. I missed our strolls, how he'd hold my hand in church, and the stability and wisdom he brought into our marriage. He exuded strength and godly character.

I grabbed my Bible, opened to Deuteronomy 31, and read about Moses when he told the people of Israel, he would not cross the Jordan River into the Promised Land with them. The Lord would go before them, along with

Joshua.

Verse 6 brought me hope. "Be strong and courageous. Do not be afraid or terrified because of them, for the LORD your God goes with you. He will never leave you nor forsake you."

I believed I'd found my purpose at BCH—to help Blake find hope and healing. I prayed for guidance and for Chad's visit the following day. I wasn't ready for my employment there to end.

~

The next morning, a Friday, I repeated, "I am strong, intelligent, and a fighter—not a quitter," on my drive to the office.

When I arrived at my desk, I checked my email. The day got a little brighter. Blake had emailed me saying, "All-day conference today. Won't be in. I'll expect an account of what you accomplish today in my absence."

He sent it at 5:00 a.m. Why wasn't the conference on his calendar?

Tauni waltzed in. "Is Blake here?" She paraded to his office door and peeked inside, then sulked back to my desk and pursed her lips. "I need to see him."

"He's at a conference in town."

Her eyes widened, and she raised her eyebrows. "And you weren't invited to go along? Did he take someone else? Debra told me she always accompanied him to conferences and meetings away from the office. She took notes and networked for the company."

"He didn't need anyone today." I faced my monitor. I assumed she had finished her jabs and would be on her way.

"Maybe you're not meeting his expectations. I'll offer my services next time." She strutted out with her nose in the air.

She's another one in need of Your love and hope, isn't she? Could you give me someone easy?

Around 4:00 p.m., with extra time on my hands, I strolled into Blake's office to get a better view of the roses painting. The gifted artist captured intricate detail in each petal. The painting included one blemished rose. The rest were perfect. In the bottom right-hand corner was the name, C. Conner. I presumed that was his deceased wife, Cheryl. I touched a petal.

"Ms. Reynolds."

I jumped.

Blake drew out my name like my dad used to do when I was in trouble as a kid.

I trembled, my elbow hit the bookcase to my left, and I stumbled.

He hurried past me, almost knocking me over. He rescued a vase that was teetering on the top shelf and glared at me. "Leave. Now."

I hated that he used a scolding tone. I wasn't a child.

He carried the bud vase over to the windows that overlooked our parking lot. He stood there and stared out. "Don't ever snoop in my office again."

My chin quivered. He thought I was a snoop. He could write me up. Nothing was in my record like that. If I apologized, I'd be admitting a mistake. But I didn't snoop. I admired.

I spun on my heels and bolted out of his office toward my desk while I rubbed my elbow. At some point, I must have done something horrific for him to have this much animosity toward me. *I can't fix this.* The verse from the night before entered my mind. *Be strong. Don't be afraid. God is with you.*

A few minutes later, Blake came out of his office and left without speaking to me. Why did he come back when he said he'd be gone all day?

Shortly before I left for home, Chad paid me his promised visit.

I stiffened. Did Blake tell him I was trouble and a snoop? Friday afternoons were the perfect time for a company to terminate someone.

"I stopped over to see how you're doing."

My mouth went dry. "Good."

"How's your elbow?"

"My elbow?" I tried to hide it from his view. But he walked around my desk to get a glimpse. "I'm fine." I spun in my chair to face him and hoped he'd give up.

"Appears bruised. I'll go to the break room and get you some ice." He strolled back to the front of my desk.

"Please don't fuss over me. I can get ice." I rubbed my arm. "How did you know about my elbow?"

"Blake called me. He was concerned about you."

I stifled my laugh and looked down until he spoke again.

"He asked me to check on you." Chad smiled. "He said you'd been in his office—"

"Snooping?"

"He did say snooping." Chad sat across from me and leaned back.

I told Chad I'd gone into Blake's office to get a better look at the beautiful painting. Not to snoop.

"I believe you." He nodded. "If it makes you feel any better, Blake told me yesterday you're an excellent assistant."

What a joke. I wanted to say that but didn't want to do anything that would be considered disloyal to my boss. I peeked at my watch. "Time for me to go home." I took my purse out of the drawer and stood.

Chad jumped up. "Anytime you want to talk about your work conditions, know that I'm available to listen. Blake's my friend, but you're an important part of our team. I want to know if things become too much for you to handle."

He must know how difficult Blake can be. "I appreciate your concern, but everything's fine." I hoped I sounded positive, although I didn't feel that way at that moment. Chad's persistence made me uneasy. He spoke with sincerity and sounded genuine. But did he expect me to tattle on my boss? I had faith that God was with me and working everything out. I avoided Chad's eyes and moved my purse to the other shoulder.

"If you're not comfortable talking to me, then talk with Beth. I know you're friends, and that might be easier for you. She'll tell me what she feels I should know. Or, you can always take your concerns to Miranda Franks in HR."

"No problems." I faked a smile.

"Blake's struggling right now." Chad spoke in a soothing tone. "I'd like to support him, but I don't approve of the way he takes his frustration out on you. And that's what's happening here." He sighed. "I know yesterday was tough."

I closed my eyes for a moment and held onto the edge of my desk. When I opened them, I tilted my head and shrugged. "You know what's going on?"

"Blake and I meet and talk regularly. We've known each other for years."

"Some days are harder than others. They're not all terrible." I kept my tone even. "Today was good until an hour ago." I raised my eyebrows.

Chad smiled and rubbed the back of his neck. "Maybe one day soon, he'll be able to explain everything to you. But it's not my story to tell."

I nodded. "I appreciate you sharing this with me."

On my drive home, I tried to process Chad's visit. What was up with Blake? Me—a great assistant? And what justified his frustration toward me?

Three

On Monday morning while I prepared breakfast, I asked the Lord to help me share His love and hope at work, as well as for boldness.

When I arrived at the office, I opened my email to find one from Blake that he'd sent an hour earlier.

"Although Marketing usually sets up my conference travel, I would like you to make all the arrangements to a healthcare conference in mid-November. We will be attending this year's annual conference in Albuquerque, New Mexico. Check with Marketing for the rest of the information."

I didn't understand his email. Who are "we"? BCH? Or *we* as in him and me? Surely not.

I called the senior administrative assistant in Marketing. After we chatted for a minute, I said, "Do you know who plans to attend the Albuquerque conference with Blake?"

"He said you were."

"Me? Is that the normal procedure?"

"Debra attended. She always seemed to enjoy it."

"Oh really?" *This will never work.* "What did Debra do at the conference?"

"She manned the exhibit booth, and there's a banquet you may want to attend. The conference offers tours to see the city sights if you decide to go. Blake will be busy. You'll want to plan to do things without him. I'm sure you'll enjoy it. I'll forward you an email with the details."

We ended the call.

Enjoy traveling with my boss who seemed to hate me? That would be a lot of together time. I wasn't comfortable with the idea.

From where I sat, I had a clear view of Blake's desk and him. He was busy at his computer. I got up and knocked on his door. "I'd like to speak to you about the conference travel arrangements you asked me to make."

"Have a seat. I'll be right with you."

I sat in the chair across from his desk.

After a few more keystrokes, he leaned back and twisted his chair toward me. He pulled out his cell and stared at it. "What information do you need?"

I rubbed my hands together in my lap. "I'm happy to make your travel arrangements, but I'm not sure I can attend."

He looked up and placed his phone on his desk. "Why not?" He folded his arms across his chest.

"I may have plans that weekend. I'll need to verify my calendar. Wouldn't it be better if I took care of office matters while you're away?"

He leaned toward me. "I'll need someone with me. I can't be in the sessions and oversee our booth at the same time. If you can't arrange to go, check with Tauni. She'll be happy to attend."

"Tauni, sir? Are you sure?" I glanced over to the roses painting and then back at Blake. "I'll try to find you someone else."

"Tauni or you. You decide." He spun his chair

toward his monitor. "Makes no difference to me."

"Yes, sir."

I stood and dashed out of his office. *Tauni? Do I dare send her with him? Or is it okay for me to go?*

I needed to prepare a statistical spreadsheet, but I found it hard to focus on such a detailed task. I put the information off to the side of my desk and darted into the file room to continue the filing from last week.

While I filed, I couldn't get the thought of spending all that time with Blake out of my head. I didn't want to attend with him. What a horrible way to spend four days, including my weekend.

When I returned to my desk, I called Beth to see if she had lunch plans. We've talked regularly since I moved to the fourth floor. We had a lot in common. However, I hadn't shared much with her about my struggles with Blake. Time to heed Chad's advice and discuss my troubles with her.

We agreed to have lunch at a deli shop nearby and met in her office at 11:30. She looked cute in her flowery maxi skirt and turquoise top. Colorful beads and silver chains hung from her neck. Her short auburn hair glistened in the sunlight, and her large dark brown eyes shone as she told me about her grandson's progress in school.

While we walked to the restaurant, I asked about the rest of her family. After listening to her answer, I finally got around to my real reason for asking her to lunch. "Blake wants me to accompany him to a conference in a couple of months, and I'm not comfortable with the idea. Should I be concerned?"

"I know the two of you have experienced tough times, but this could be an opportunity for you to get to know him in a relaxed setting. I think it will be good for both of you."

"But what will Tauni say? She'll make a big deal out of it."

"You can't worry about her. Tauni's going to be Tauni. What other choices do you have?"

"He said I could go, or she could go."

"You, my friend, have a dilemma on your hands. Tauni would love to get her paws on Blake."

A horn honked and a man in a BMW waved as he drove past.

I touched Beth's arm. "Was that Blake?"

She nodded. "Nice of him to say hello, don't you think?"

"He waved at you. Not me." I looked down at the sidewalk. "Is it my responsibility to keep Tauni away? I'm not Blake's protector."

"In a way, you may be his protector. And maybe the Lord put you here 'for such a time as this.'"

I placed my hand on my chest. "Now I'm Queen Esther?"

"Perhaps you are. God brought you here for a reason."

We arrived at the deli and stood in line. I scanned the menu on the wall and decided on a turkey and avocado sandwich. Beth ordered the broccoli cheddar soup. We brushed crumbs off a table in the corner and waited for our food. Service was slow. We had to gulp down our meal to get back to the office on time.

On the walk back, I asked Beth about Blake's wife. "She died in a car accident?"

"Yes. Tragic."

"He's often demanding and rude with me, like he's

pushing me away. Do you think I remind him of Cheryl?"

"Possibly." She looked behind her and lowered her voice. "He still struggles with her death. He's had a difficult time with it. I heard Friday afternoon was rough."

"Did Chad tell you?"

"He shared a little. Certain events set Blake off."

A group of people approached from the opposite direction. We formed a single file line with Beth in front.

But why does he take those events out on me?

After they passed, I rushed ahead to join Beth. "Did Cheryl die this time of year?"

"No. Early March. But Friday was Blake's daughter's birthday." Beth offered a deep sigh. "Family celebrations without Cheryl have always been difficult for him."

"Hard to lose loved ones. Maybe a counselor could help."

"I don't know. I've been concerned about him for a while. He's a great guy. I hope you get to find out for yourself one day soon."

We arrived at the office a few minutes early, despite the slow service.

I followed Beth to her desk where we continued our conversation. "Life has been tough since Sam died. I depended on him for so much. But the Lord helps me through."

I heard someone behind me. Blake. He came out of Chad's office and slipped by us without speaking. I looked back at Beth. "How would you describe the sound he made? A grunt?"

"Or possibly a snicker. Do you suppose he didn't

agree with what you said about the Lord helping you?"

"Probably. I'd like to know what goes on in his head."

"Hang in there." She took a seat and jiggled her computer mouse.

I excused myself and strolled across the hall. Blake stood near the copier. I ambled up next to him. "Is there anything I can help you with?" I kept my tone light and positive.

He glanced at me. "I'm good."

"My workload isn't that heavy this afternoon. Other than your spreadsheet, I'm available if you have something extra I can do for you."

He stopped making his copies and focused on me. "How long ago did you lose your husband?"

I think I heard a tiny bit of compassion. "Three years ago. Heart failure."

"Was he a lot older than you?"

"A few years."

Blake took his copies out of the tray. He was back in business mode, staring at his printouts. "So, who will attend the conference with me?"

"May I let you know tomorrow?"

"Yes." He fed a few more sheets of paper through without taking his eyes off the copier. "How's your elbow? I asked Chad to check on you Friday. Did he?"

"A little sore, but I'm fine. He checked on me before I left."

Blake strode back into his office without an apology.

To at least try to smooth things between us, I needed to swallow my pride and ask him to forgive me for being in his office. I stood outside his door to gather my resolve before I entered. When I walked in, he stood staring out the window and didn't know I was there. "I owe you an apology."

"You owe *me* an apology?" He looked at me with wide eyes.

I nodded. "Although I didn't snoop, I was in your office without a good reason Friday. I wanted to get a closer look at your wife's painting—something personal to you. I didn't intend any disrespect. I'm sorry if I hurt or upset you in any way."

He moved toward his desk and sat. He picked up one of the copies he'd made and stared at it. "You did nothing wrong. I was out of line. Now, if you'll excuse me, I have things I must do."

"Yes, sir." I darted back to my desk. How could he admit he was wrong but couldn't apologize?

An email from Beth popped up on my computer screen. "We plan to have a retirement party for Ross Jacoby from Marketing in two weeks. The assistants from his department and Tauni have helped me with a few things, but I could use your help with some of the last-minute details if you have time."

I shot back a quick response. "I'd love to help. What do you need me to do?"

We coordinated back and forth, and I took on a couple of specific tasks in preparation for the party.

I then checked off completed items on my to-do list. I still needed to do the statistical spreadsheet. But I didn't think it would take the rest of the afternoon.

I looked for a previous month's report but couldn't find it on our server. I rushed into the file room for the hard copy. When I came out, I planned to check with Blake one more time to see if he needed help with anything else.

His office door was partially closed. I heard Chad say, "I think you should make sure she knows she'd be welcomed at Ross's party. I think it might be good for the two of you to get to know each other in a casual setting. Smooth things out between you."

I didn't need to hear Chad discussing Blake's personal life. I started to walk back to my desk but paused when Blake responded.

"I'm not so desperate that I need to invite my assistant to a party. I know many *beautiful* women who'd be happy to accompany me."

I raced to my desk and slouched into my chair. I had no desire to be anywhere with that man, especially with the way he talked down to me. He basically said that if he invited me to the party, it would be an act of desperation. I shook my head.

Let it go. He's Blake.

Four

I enjoyed a quiet evening at home, which is exactly what I needed after a frustrating day with Blake. After dinner, I made a batch of brownies and put them in the oven. Roxie, my orange tabby, and I settled down on the living room sofa. Her purr calmed me a little. At least one of us was content. I didn't experience this turmoil when working in IT. My biggest problem was Wes. He would ask me to lunch often, and I didn't want to date. Since working for Blake, there seemed to be constant drama. And knowing I was a part of it didn't ease my anxiety.

I turned to Esther 4 to research "for such a time as this." As the queen, Esther was where God needed her to be to bring hope and deliverance to her people. I grabbed my journal off the coffee table to make notes but put it down again without writing anything. *Should I travel with Blake on this business trip or allow Tauni to attend?*

After a few minutes of prayer, I needed confirmation and wise counsel. I retrieved my phone from the kitchen counter and called my small group leader from church, Manuel Gallegos. He answered on the third ring.

"I need advice," I said after our normal greeting. "My boss wants me to travel with him to Albuquerque for a conference in November. Would it be wrong for me to accompany him?"

I paced while I waited for Manuel's reply. I knew him well. He would ask the Lord for a response.

"If you think he has inappropriate intentions for you, don't go. If attending is a part of your job, his normal way to do things, and you feel comfortable, go."

"I've been told his former assistant traveled with him often. Must be normal." I checked the timer for my brownies—less than one minute remained. "But God's Word says to reject every kind of evil. Won't this look bad to people? We're both widowed." The timer beeped. I managed to get the brownies out with one hand and not burn myself. "I don't want anyone to think there's something between us."

"It's God who counts. He knows the truth. Maybe your presence there will make a huge impact on your boss. God may be calling you 'for such a time as this.'"

I pulled my shoulders back, moved the phone from my ear, and stared at it. *Again? What are you trying to tell me, Lord?*

We ended our call a few minutes later.

Manuel did say if I felt comfortable, then I should go. I still wasn't happy with the idea. What if Blake and I bickered with one another the whole trip? What if he continued to scold me like a child? But maybe God would use me like He used Esther. Instead of deliverance for the Jews, perhaps hope and deliverance would come to Blake.

~

I awoke early the next morning after a restless night. I needed to decide. After my devotions and a prayer for clarity, I got ready to go into the office. I would be an hour early. I hoped to make all the Albuquerque arrangements before Blake arrived.

I got to my desk at 7:00 a.m. and made our airline reservations, booked the hotel rooms, reserved a car, and registered us for the conference. Would Blake be surprised, pleased, or disappointed that I planned to attend instead of Tauni?

He would arrive soon to meet with Chad for their weekly check-in. I rushed to the break room, poured him a cup of coffee, and placed it on his desk, hoping that was something Blake would appreciate.

Before I left his office, he entered. I didn't want him to think I was there to snoop again. "I brought you a cup of coffee."

He peered at his desk. "You forgot the cream."

"I thought you drank it black. I'll be right back." I hurried out of his office and almost got run over by Tauni on her way in to see Blake.

What is she wearing? I hadn't seen such a low-cut top since the last time I ventured to the beach. And what was up with her micro miniskirt?

I whisked myself over to Blake's door, which Tauni closed after slinking inside. I knocked and entered. "Blake, I wanted to remind you of your 8:30 a.m. meeting with Chad." I spoke in my sweetest tone. "I believe he's already expecting you."

He raised his eyebrows. "I appreciate the reminder." He focused on Tauni. "Unless Keedryn has decided to attend the conference with me, I have no problem if you attend in her place."

Conference? She breezed into his office dressed like that to ask him if she could accompany him to the conference?

"Oh, Tauni, I finalized reservations for Blake and

me earlier this morning." I glanced at Blake and caught his nonreaction. At least he didn't frown.

"Well then," she said with her eyes ablaze, "I guess I should get back to work."

Blake and Tauni left his office together. I followed them out. He left our suite and strode across the hall to Chad's office. She turned down the hallway to the right. I assumed to catch the elevator.

After Blake was out of sight, Tauni returned. "You tramp. How dare you decide to go on this trip when you found out I want to go. Blake would much rather have my company than yours, and you know it. You can't handle the truth, can you? You're dull and unattractive. You can't make him interested in you, no matter how hard you try."

I took a step back, stunned by her abruptness. "I don't know why you're so determined to hate me." I took a few steps to my chair and caught my foot on the wheels underneath. I grabbed hold of my desk to keep my balance, straightened, took a deep breath, and placed my hands on my hips. "The reservations are made. I'll accompany Blake. I'm his executive assistant. Not you. No personal agenda. I'm just doing my job. Nothing more." My tone was sharp.

Her gaze went to the ceiling and back. "This isn't over."

My hands trembled after losing it with her. *This stupid chair.* I wanted to be sweet and show love and acceptance, but I blew it big time.

Blake loped past my desk. "I'd like to see you in my office."

I stiffened. "Yes, sir. Do I need my notepad?"

"No. Only you."

What now, Lord? I didn't need Blake's attitude too. Why did he come back right away? Was I the topic of this week's discussion with Chad? Would I be fired? Or maybe Blake wanted Tauni to go with him instead of me. She was attractive and outgoing—valuable attributes at an exhibit booth. I stared at my computer monitor.

He called to me from his doorway. "Did you get lost?"

"No, sir," I stammered. "I'm on my way."

I stepped inside, and he closed the door—something he rarely did, which made me feel uncomfortable.

"Have a seat." He gestured to the four chairs at his round table.

I sat, and he took a chair across from me.

"What's going on?" he asked.

"What? You mean when I told you about your appointment with Chad?"

"You barged in here and told me about an appointment with Chad that had been canceled. He took the morning off. You watch my calendar. I think you knew that."

"I didn't know what to think. Tauni flew by me and waltzed into your office. She knows she should stop and talk to me first. I felt like I needed to protect you or something."

"Protect me? You don't think I can handle the likes of Tauni Fisher?"

I sighed. "She doesn't dress unprofessionally on a regular basis. I thought maybe you could use my help to get her to follow company policies."

He rubbed his forehead. "Let me get this straight. She walked by you looking unprofessional." He paused and wrinkled his nose. "You thought if you came in here, you could help me get her to follow company guidelines?"

"She slithered by me." I bit my lip to keep a giggle at bay. His expression and my comments sounded ridiculous, even to me. "However, when you put it the way you have, it doesn't make much sense, does it? I'd better get back to work." I pushed my chair away from the table.

"Not so fast." He lifted his palm. "I have a theory about what happened here."

"I suppose you plan to share it with me?" I clamped my mouth shut. Better if I didn't respond any further.

"I find it rather entertaining but hard to understand after the way I treated you on Friday." He leaned toward me. "I believe, Ms. Reynolds, you are jealous of Ms. Fisher."

I stared at him. *Did he say jealous?* And did he think he only treated me poorly on Friday? I was not, nor would I ever be jealous of Tauni or any involvement she may have with that . . . that arrogant man. "What leads you to believe I'm jealous?" My response was calm, even though I was not.

"I think you came in here to make sure she kept things professional. You didn't want her to act in an inappropriate manner to get her own way." He leaned back and crossed his legs.

He's smiling. He thinks this is humorous. I frowned. "I'm a mother and a grandmother. I protect those I care about. I felt you needed to be protected. If you wish to call it jealousy, so be it." I flung my hand in a "whatever" gesture and stood.

"Thank you, K. Since Neil is Tauni's manager, I'll ask him to remind her of our company's guidelines."

Blake chuckled and picked up his coffee cup. "I still need my cream."

I shivered. I didn't like that he'd called me K. That wasn't my name. I hurried back to the break room for a packet of cream and a fresh cup of coffee. The first one must have been cold by now.

I'd prayed for a smile and got one. But me, jealous?

~

I asked Beth to join me on a walk during our morning break. I needed to let off some steam, and the day was beautiful and sunny. We strolled along the meandering path that surrounded the duck pond on BCH property. I loved this park-like setting. So peaceful and a great place to relax. And with a few of the leaves starting to change, it was the perfect place for a stroll.

"I protect those I care about? Why in the world did I say such a thing?" I rambled while Beth listened. "What does he think I meant? What did I mean?"

"Could you be jealous?"

"I'm not jealous of Tauni or anyone else. I'm not interested in Blake, except as his assistant. I have no romantic interest. None."

A mallard landed in the pond and splashed in the water.

"If you're not jealous, and you're not interested in him, then don't worry about it. I think you're making something out of nothing."

"But if I don't care, why did I say I did?"

"You do care. God, who lives in you, cares. It doesn't have to mean anything more. Blake will think you're a kind and thoughtful person who looks out for her boss's best interests."

I nodded. "I have his best interests at heart. Nothing

more. But he still thinks I'm jealous."

"I'm sure this isn't the first time he's been wrong."

"He smiled at me. That tells you something."

"He smiled?"

"He found my jealousy amusing."

Beth clasped her hands together. "God used you to get him to smile. Don't you see? Go with it. You may be the one God uses to heal Blake's broken heart. I'm so excited."

"Excited? He thinks I like him."

"Maybe that's a part of God's plan too." She cocked her head and grinned.

"No."

Beth's eyes grew wide. "No?"

I moaned. "His smile lit up his entire face. And with those blue eyes." I stared out over the pond and then looked at Beth. "Why are you laughing at me?"

"Not interested, huh?" She beamed and gave me an all-knowing nod.

"I think I'd better call HR and get a transfer out. I'm sure Tauni would love to make her move to my desk."

"Yes, if at first you don't succeed."

"What do you mean?"

"Tauni applied for your position. She can't stand the thought that she didn't get it and you did. Why do you think she's bent on getting back at you?"

"I thought she was after Blake."

"I think it's probably more about making you miserable."

"She has become a pain." I glanced at my watch. "Time to head back. Thanks for listening to me ramble."

Back at my desk after my fifteen-minute break, I struggled to concentrate on my tasks, given that Blake thought I was attracted to him. I needed to get a signature on a letter he asked me to prepare, but I didn't want to take it into his office. I straightened the things on my desk and dusted off the picture frames. When I ran out of ways to stall, I took the letter in and handed it to him.

After he signed it, he leaned back in his chair and grinned. He was still smiling about this, which wasn't like him.

"You're enjoying this aren't you?" I shifted my weight to the opposite leg.

"I'm flattered you feel you need to look out for me. Debra had my back, too, but I didn't expect you to follow in her footsteps. To show her my appreciation, I'd often invite her to lunch. Would you join me today?"

"Not necessary." I stared out his window. I didn't want to see his eyes. "I already have plans." I returned his gaze. "Thank you though." I hoped he didn't notice my voice crack.

"Maybe another time."

I raised my eyebrows. "How would it look to others? Like a date? We can't do that."

"Whoa." Blake lifted both palms to me and shook his head. "I didn't ask you on a date."

"Of course, you didn't." My hands shook. I clasped them behind my back. "I know that. But other people might *think* we're on a date."

His eyes narrowed. "You do realize that when we're in Albuquerque, no one here will know when we have dinner together. Unless the company sends spies to follow us. Maybe we should eat at different restaurants." He grinned. He found enjoyment in making fun of me.

"We can eat together in Albuquerque, since it won't be a date." I spun to leave and nearly knocked Tauni over.

"Did I hear the two of you are going on a date?"

I could imagine my face turning deep shades of red. "No, Tauni, you misunderstood. We've had this conversation before. I'm not about to have it again." I hated to walk away. What if she asked Blake out? I stood along the wall just inside his office door where I could observe their interaction.

She put on a sweet face to make me look like the villain. Her southern charm and fake smile didn't help my case.

"Blake, I was asked to deliver this envelope to you right away. And if you need a fun date," she winked at him, "I'm your woman." With a tilt of her head, along with a flirtatious glance and sway of her hips, she swaggered away. She wrinkled her nose at me on her way out.

I stared at Blake with my mouth open. *She was totally out of line.*

Blake twisted away from me and bent his head down. "Maybe I should take her up on that offer." He picked up his coffee cup, then set it back down. "I need to get out more." He turned back around but kept his eyes on his desk with his hand covering his mouth.

I tilted my head and scowled. "Maybe you should." Was that a smirk on his face? I turned toward the door but stopped and looked over my shoulder. "Would you prefer she travels to Albuquerque with you as well?"

His head shot up, and his eyes grew wide. "Not really." He stood. "I plan to write her up and not involve Neil. In addition to her attire, her actions and comments were extremely inappropriate just now." He spoke in a serious tone.

I took a step toward his desk. "I agree." But what about his comment regarding taking her up on her offer? Was he just trying to annoy me?

He lowered his eyes. "I believe this will be a good trip for both of us. I look forward to it."

I shook my head and made my exit without another word. I did, however, hear him say, "Yep. Jealousy."

Yep. Arrogance.

38

Five

After lunch, I worked on a departmental report Blake had written and reviewed several financial spreadsheets.

He stepped out of his office and came over to my desk. "I need the report now. Chad asked to review it."

A day filled with smiles is about to turn ugly. "I've edited the text part, but I haven't checked all the spreadsheets."

"You've had all day. What takes you so long? Debra would have had it done this morning."

I pulled my hand away from my mouse. "I liked Debra. She was always nice to me when I brought you reports from IT. But I'm not her." I stood and darted to the front of my desk. Sick and tired of confrontations with Tauni and comparisons to Debra, I was ready to battle. My eyes met his. "Maybe she's had second thoughts and wishes she hadn't retired. If you call her, maybe she'll come back and work for you another ten years. Or I'll be happy to call her for you."

He chuckled. I supposed he was happy because he planned to fire me for speaking to him in an unprofessional manner.

"You're spunky today. First with Tauni and now me. I'll try to back off and give you some space and not compare you to Aunt Debra. Her mind's still sharp at seventy, but who knows what it will be like in ten years."

"Aunt Debra?" My jaw dropped open.

"My mother's sister. Not common knowledge here. I'd say most people have no idea."

I returned to my computer, printed off a fresh copy of the report he needed for Chad, and retrieved it from the printer. I placed it in Blake's outstretched hand. "I'm sorry I spoke harshly. I had no right."

He remained close to me. "You had every right," he said in a soft tone. "I know I tend to be a little demanding and set in my ways." He proceeded across the hall.

A little demanding? No, Blake. No little about it.

I finished for the day and drove home. What a day it had been. Blake smiled, chuckled, and invited me to lunch. I kind of liked these new traits. Except, he was still arrogant and thought I was slow.

After dinner that evening, I opened my Bible and read from Joshua 6—the story about the walls of Jericho tumbling down. Joshua must have looked foolish to the people of Jericho. But he obeyed and trusted God. He was a man of tremendous faith.

I stared across my living room. *If I get remarried, I want a man like Joshua.*

Remarried? Where did that come from? I was perfectly content. Me and my cat.

My thoughts turned to Blake. I found it funny that Debra was Blake's aunt. My grin turned to a frown though when I realized that he didn't travel to conferences with his executive assistant. He traveled with his aunt.

~

On Wednesday morning, Blake was in another bad

mood. He waltzed over to my desk and shook his head. "I can't believe you gave me this letter to sign when it looks like this."

I stood and tried to take the letter from his flailing arm. He kept moving it out of my reach.

"And what's up with the filing? I tried to find a folder in the file room and everything's in shambles. Look at how things are done and follow the same pattern. You don't need to redo all the processes already in place. I can't find anything."

I opened my mouth to interrupt. But he was on a roll and wouldn't stop.

"And why can't you keep up? Do you need to attend a training workshop on organizational skills or time management? I can make it happen for you."

I needed to reign in my feelings, speak with respect, and not lose it, again. *Lord, help me to keep my tone soft.* "Please tell me what I did that's upset you. Show me the letter, and tell me which file you need. I'll find it for you."

Without another word, he stormed back to his office and slammed the door.

I shrugged and rubbed my forehead. I needed a change of scenery and trudged to the restroom.

Beth followed me in and hugged me. "I heard him from across the hall. You're a remarkable assistant. You know you are. Something must have set him off. Not you."

"Always me. I have no idea why. Yesterday, we made progress. Today he's treated me like a child. I need to see Miranda. Maybe she knows of another position opening soon. I don't know how much longer I can take this."

"You got him to smile. Hold onto that. Blake needs you. He fights inner battles over Cheryl's death, and for some reason, he feels comfortable taking his hurt out on you."

"Thanks. I'm so encouraged." I slumped down onto the pale green sofa just inside the ladies' room.

Beth took a seat next to me. "I know what might help."

I sat up straight.

"Have you thought about talking to Debra? She thought highly of you, and I'm sure she'd love to talk. I'll email you her number." She patted my leg. "I've got to get back to my desk. Please let me know if I can help in any way."

Beth hurried off. I needed to get back to my desk too. But what about Debra? I'd thought about calling her a couple of times over the past few months. Did I dare try? She was Blake's aunt and would be partial to him. I needed to give that some thought.

~

A busy Thursday consisted of reports, letters, meetings, and minutes. Blake gave me the silent treatment. No apologies. No smiles. Not even a thank you for anything. At our afternoon break, Beth and I escaped to Starbucks across the street to talk about our progress with the retirement party.

"I love coming in here." I took a deep breath. "I enjoy the smell of brewed coffee, even though I don't drink the stuff straight. The best I can do is a café mocha. I need my chocolate."

"Me too. I'm always tempted by the chocolate pops. Can't get enough of those."

Beth reminded me of the way Nicki pointed at her

favorites.

I scanned the menu. "Do you know what kind of coffee Blake likes?"

"I think he gets the Pike Place."

"I want to order him one and surprise him. But I don't know if he'll want cream or not. I haven't figured out his pattern yet."

"He's rather finicky about his cream. Grab one when we get back. He can decide if he wants it or not. And if you want to kill him with kindness, I know he likes their brownies too."

"I'll get one of those. I don't know what I did. He won't speak to me."

"He probably feels terrible about the way he talked to you yesterday." Beth put a hand on my shoulder. "I'm sorry you have to go through this."

We ordered our drinks and the brownie and discussed the party while we waited for the barista to call our names. On our walk back to the office, Beth invited me to a women's conference at her church in mid-October—four weeks away. I told her yes. I yearned for wisdom and strength as soon as possible on how to deal with Blake. Despite a few good moments here and there, things were not going well between us.

I zipped to the break room and picked up a creamer packet. Inside our suite, I poked my head into Blake's office. "Do you have a moment?"

"What do you need?" Sounded like one long word.

"Nothing. I wanted to bring you an afternoon treat. I hope you like it."

I set the coffee and bag with the brownie on his desk and returned to mine. I didn't hear anything from him again until 4:55 p.m.—five minutes before I was supposed to leave for the day. He sent me an email: "I need this letter finalized. Now."

The link included in the email led me to the letter he needed. Ended up being five pages of text to proof, plus, he wanted me to review two spreadsheets.

I entered his office. "I'm just about off for the day. Can the letter wait until morning?"

He stared at his monitor. "I need it before you leave."

"I'll get it to you as quickly as I can." I rushed to my desk and started on his request.

Why did he wait until quitting time? *I should go in there and tell him I'm not doing this. I'm going home.* But instead, like an obedient servant, I stayed and finished the task.

Six

On Saturday morning, I awoke excited about my birthday. I looked forward to spending time with Jenny, Carl, and Nicki for dinner. I studied myself in the mirror. Time for a makeover. I'd earned it. Fortunately, I'd already scheduled a hair appointment. I needed to cover the gray that was creeping in and get a trim.

My chin-length, light brown hair turned out cute with blonde highlights. I strolled around the mall and found one of those ladies who does makeovers. She did a magnificent job. I left there $183.00 poorer.

Before I left the mall, I bought a jazzy floral skirt and a navy-blue sweater set—a perfect outfit for my birthday dinner.

At 6:30 p.m., I arrived at Jenny and Carl's. A royal blue corvette was parked in the driveway. Who could that belong to? Carl couldn't afford a car like that on his salary.

Carl worked as a children's pastor at New Life Community Church in Brentwood, and Jenny didn't work a regular job. She finished college and received her teaching degree after Nicki was born. For the past three years, she'd been a stay-at-home mom and helped Carl with activities at church. With Nicki in kindergarten,

Jenny often worked as a tutor and substitute teacher.

Nicki met me at the door. "Wait till you see the pretty flowers. Someone likes you a bunch." She bounced up and down and clapped her hands.

"What flowers? Are they from your parents?"

"They came for you today. A man in a delivery truck brought them. They're the most awesome flowers I've ever seen in my life. Mama said they're from Montel's. She said rich people buy from there, and poor people like us can't afford it."

Jenny met me in the hallway. "I guess Nicki told you? They arrived—"

"Is this the birthday girl?" A man I didn't recognize with a huge grin joined us in the foyer and stuck out his hand.

"And you are?" I shook his hand.

"Dan. I'm a friend of Jenny and Carl's from church. We're in the same small group."

I pulled off my jacket and glared at Jenny. She'd talked often in recent months about fixing me up with a blind date—something she knew I didn't want her to do.

Jenny took my jacket. "Dan stopped by to check on Nicki. She wasn't feeling well last night when we met with our group from church."

"I feel better today." Nicki grabbed my hand. "You don't have to worry 'bout me."

I glanced down at Nicki. "Do I smell your daddy's lasagna?"

"Yep. And he fixed the cake you like too."

Carl joined us in the foyer and hugged me. "I see you've met Dan. I asked him to stay for dinner. I hope you don't mind."

"Not at all." I looked from Carl to Dan. "Welcome.

Nice to have you join us."

Dan's grin grew wider. He and Carl strode into the kitchen to check on the garlic bread while Jenny complimented me on my hair, makeup, and new outfit.

She took after Sam's side of the family. Dark brown hair, brown eyes, and a small build. We were about the same height, but she was in much better shape. She lost her baby fat after Nicki was born—probably because she loved to run—and kept it off. I couldn't make that claim.

Carl and Jenny made a cute couple. His hair and eye color matched hers. Although, he towered over her by at least ten inches. He played basketball in high school and earned a college scholarship.

Nicki had the same dark brown hair and eyes as her parents. She was a beauty.

"Now, where are those flowers, Nicki?" I released my hand from hers and ran my fingers through her long flowing curls.

Jenny took my arm and whispered, "They're upstairs in the bonus room. I thought you might want privacy. I don't know who knew you'd be here tonight."

"Come on, Nana. I'll go with you." Nicki took my hand again and led me down the hall, past the bedrooms, dining room, kitchen, and through the living room to the stairway.

The upstairs included a spare bedroom and full-sized bathroom as well as the bonus room. Often used for church gatherings, the bonus room housed two chairs, a sectional couch, a desk and computer, a large-screen television, and a table with chairs for card and board games.

The aroma of fresh-cut roses filled my nostrils when I entered the room. I smelled their subtle fragrance before I saw them. They sat on a square coffee table in the middle of the room, and the sight of them took my breath away. "Nicki, I've never seen a more beautiful bouquet of roses."

"I told you. Do you know what the deep pink means?"

"Does it mean something special?

She touched a petal of one of the roses. "Mama looked it up. The deep pink means you're appreciated, and he's thankful for you."

"Your mom is sure these are from a man who appreciates me? Do you know what that word means?"

"Of course. He loves you and wants to marry you."

I shook my head. "No, it doesn't." I pointed to the computer in the far corner of the room. "I think you need to look up the word."

She grabbed the card from the bouquet and ran over to the desk. "I'll look on the computer right now. How do you spell it?"

I hurried to the desk and stood behind Nicki. I found a dictionary app and slowly spelled the word. She pecked out each letter. When she finally found the definition, I read it to her. "Appreciate means to be thankful, admire, or to value something or someone."

"It sounds like he loves you."

"Give me the card and we'll figure out who the mystery person is." I opened my palm.

Jenny flew up the stairs. "Who are they from?"

"We don't know yet. Nicki told me what the color means."

"Who do you think sent them? They're exquisite."

"I have no idea." I placed my hands on Nicki's shoulders. "What did you do with the card?"

She looked on the desk and stuck out her lower lip. "I put it right here. I wonder where it went."

Jenny and I searched the computer desk, the floor, and every inch of the room where Nicki had walked since she snatched the card from the bouquet. Nowhere to be found.

Jenny placed her hands on her hips. "Nicki. Where's Nana's card? It couldn't just disappear. Did you hide it?"

"No, Mommy. I put it right here." Tears streamed down her cheeks.

I reached out and hugged her. "We'll find it, sweetie. Would you go down and tell your daddy we'll be down to eat in a couple of minutes?"

"Okay." She hugged me and scurried down the stairs.

Jenny looked at me. "I know you're dying to find out who sent these to you. Do you have any ideas? Anyone from church? Work?"

"Work? Maybe, Wes. We worked together in IT. He's asked me to lunch several times over the past couple of years. I've always said no. That would be like him, though. He's a nice guy. If I wanted to date again, he'd be a good one."

"I'll keep looking for the card and ask Carl to help me. It must be here somewhere."

My stomach growled. "I'm hungry. Let's get downstairs before the guys eat all my birthday dinner."

As we started down the stairs, I lowered my voice to a whisper. "Why is Dan here?"

"What do you mean? He stopped by to check on Nicki."

"He didn't know I'd be here?"

"Carl may have mentioned it. Blame your favorite

son-in-law."

Jenny grabbed my arm to stop me from continuing down the stairs. "Please be gracious. He wanted to meet you."

I pursed my lips. "I'm always gracious. I can't believe you did this to me. I don't like it. Not one bit."

Jenny made it sound as though Carl was to blame for Dan joining us. Carl had watched out for me in a protective way since Sam's death. If Dan was Carl's idea, I needed to give Dan a break. Carl wouldn't steer me wrong. Jenny, however, tends to be frivolous. Dan was probably as silly as she. "We've had this conversation before. I appreciate you not wanting me to be alone as I get older, but I'm fine. I promise not to burden you and your family."

"That's not fair. You know this isn't about you getting old and living with us. I want you to be happy."

"Don't you think if the Lord wants me to remarry, He'll send someone to me, and I'll know he's the right one? I did well choosing your dad, didn't I? Did you help me then? Let God take care of it, Jen."

Jenny sighed. "Okay, but if these flowers are from Wes, I want to meet him right away to see if he's worthy of you."

I shook my head and descended the remaining stairs.

~

Dan and I sat across from one another at the dining room table. He was about Sam's height, around five foot ten with a receding hairline, and medium build. Truth be told, he was nice looking. He reminded me a lot of Sam. We chatted about the weather and our respective churches. My stomach was in knots. I doubted I'd be able to eat much of anything. To know he was here to meet me and not because of Nicki made me uncomfortable.

While we talked, I understood Jenny's appreciation for Dan. He was funny, personable, and seemed kind-hearted, all of which were qualities Sam possessed. Dan owned a successful computer technology company in town. If Jenny wanted to marry me off, she'd pick someone who could take care of me, so Dan made sense. On the downside, he seemed self-centered. The more he talked, the less interest I had. He made it sound as though everything he touched turned to gold. He didn't give the Lord credit for anything.

The meal was almost over when he looked at me and said, "Tell me about the most rewarding accomplishment so far in your life."

For a moment, I thought I was in a job interview. "I'm still working on it. My goal is to hear the Lord say, 'Well done, my daughter.'"

He hesitated and nodded. "That's good."

After dinner, Jenny and I cleaned the kitchen, and the guys escaped outside to check out Dan's new wheels. He left a short time later, and I was thankful he didn't ask me for my phone number.

Jenny, Nicki, and I moved to the living room. Nicki sat on the floor with a puzzle box and dumped out the pieces.

Jenny sat in her favorite comfy chair and pulled her legs up next to her. "Wasn't he engaging? He's such a likable guy."

"Really?"

"Didn't you like him? How could you not like him?"

I took a seat across from her on the sofa. "What do you like about him?"

"He's friendly and funny. He likes people. He tells

good stories."

"Does he remind you of anyone?"

"No." She paused and scrunched up her face. "Maybe. You think Dad?"

"Your dad was a wonderful man. I miss him every day. But if I were to remarry, I don't think I'd want someone who looks and acts like him. I don't believe that would be fair to his memory or my new husband. Please let me make my own choice. Besides, I'm not ready to date."

"Then there wasn't anything wrong with him? You feel it's too soon to date?"

"Don't you think he's rather self-centered? Everything pertained to him." I sighed. "He didn't give the Lord credit for any of his blessings. He made it sound like he alone did all the right things."

I stood. "I'm going to help myself to a glass of water. Would you like one?"

Jenny followed me into the kitchen. "Maybe he was nervous and wanted to make a good impression."

"Did you already know he supports several missionaries around the world, his business jumped from five employees to fifty in three years, and about his children's accomplishments?" I grabbed two glasses from the cabinet and filled them with ice and water.

"Yes, I knew all those things."

"Did he give the Lord credit when he shared this information with you before?"

"I don't think so." Her eyebrows shot up, and she took a glass from my hand. "I'm sorry for meddling."

"Does this mean you won't do it again?"

"It doesn't mean that at all." She nudged my arm with her elbow. "You know me."

~

Later that evening, at home, I set up the Echo that Jenny and Carl gave me for my birthday. I planned to use "Alexa" as its wake-up name. After I reviewed the instructions and the available skills, my curiosity about the roses consumed my thoughts.

Who could have known I would be at Jenny's? Wes may have known the date of my birthday from years past, but he didn't know my plans for the day. Beth could have mentioned it. I did tell her. Maybe someone from church. I planned to keep my eyes opened the next day. I hoped to thank whoever gave me such a sweet and generous gift.

54

Seven

Sunday morning after the worship service and before I attended my small group, I lingered near the back of the church. I watched the single men I knew, hoping someone would ask me about my birthday. No one did.

I strolled to the classroom and hugged Manuel and his wife, Susie. I sat in the back to watch everyone. Maybe someone would mention my birthday.

Two men in the class came up to me separately before Manuel began to teach and did ask. I mentioned to each of them I received a beautiful bouquet of roses to see if either would acknowledge the gift. Neither did.

My mind wandered during Manuel's teaching. A few minutes seemed to pass when I heard him say, "I hope you all have a great week."

I checked my text messages as I darted out to my car. One from Jenny. "Found the card. You won't believe it. Come for lunch. Carl grilling burgers." What wouldn't I believe? Who sent them?

I didn't bother to ring the doorbell. I let myself in. "Jenny?"

"We're out back on the deck."

Nicki came running down the hallway and into the foyer. "Nana. Nana. I'm so glad you're here. I missed you this much." She opened her arms as wide as she could.

I reached down to give her a big hug. "I was here last night."

"You mean you didn't miss me too?" She stuck out both lips.

I chuckled, scooped her up into my arms, and stood. "I missed you so much I came back today to see you."

She giggled with glee and then squirmed.

I either had to put her down or drop her, so I opted for the former, then passed through the kitchen on my way to the deck. There, on the counter, laid my card—what was left of it. "What in the world happened here?"

According to Jenny, they found the ripped card under the dog's bed. Nicki must have dropped the card last night, and Lucy snatched it and ran.

"I'm not sure we can put this back together." I rubbed my forehead. "There must be fifty pieces here."

Nicki ran over to one of the kitchen drawers and pulled out some tape. "Only fourteen. I counted them. Is that right, Mommy?"

Exaggerations are wasted on a child.

"Yes, sweetie. Fourteen." Jenny chuckled.

Nicki handed me the tape. "I'll help you. It will be okay. We can fix it together."

I rubbed her back. "Thank you for helping." I didn't want to make her feel bad for dropping the card.

Nicki and I sat at the kitchen table and pulled the envelope off the card pieces. The dried dog slobber made it a gross task.

Jenny hurried outside to help Carl with the grill. She came inside when we started to open the card pieces.

My cell phone rang, and I peeked at the screen. "Sis.

She didn't call me yesterday and probably wants to wish me a happy birthday." I stood.

"We've got this." Jenny took my seat next to Nicki. "You talk to Auntie Viv. We'll keep working."

I answered the phone and strolled to the guest bedroom at the front of the house to talk. I was gone for about fifteen minutes. When I returned to the kitchen, the card was somewhat mended. Had a few holes, but it could have been worse.

Nicki jumped up and down. "He knows what the color means. He wants to marry you. Read it to her, Mommy."

"Nicki, that's silly." I plopped down on a kitchen chair.

"Yay." Nicki danced with glee. "I'm going to have a new Papa." She sprinted out the back door to Carl.

Jenny laughed as she watched Nicki run to her daddy. "It looks like we're missing an important part of the card. The part with his name. But there should be enough here for you to know who sent them. I'll read exactly what I see."

"'Thanks for putting . . . me. I . . . to know how . . . appreciate you . . . thankful you're . . . and I look forward to . . . together.'"

"That makes no sense. Let me see the handwriting."

Jenny handed the card to me. I gasped.

"What? Who?"

I covered my mouth. "No. Can't be. What in the world?" I shook my head and lowered my hand. "Blake Conner. My boss."

"The mean guy who doesn't appreciate a thing you do?"

"Yes." I squeaked out the word.

"I think you're wrong about him. Looks like he thinks the world of you. Has he asked you out yet?"

I stood and began to pace. "No. Yes. Well, kind of, I guess. He asked me to go to lunch with him last week." I stopped and looked at Jenny. "Wipe that smile off your face, dear. I told him no."

"Why?"

"First of all, he's my boss, and then there's the fact that he's mean and cranky." I placed my hands on my hips. "Why would I want to go to lunch with him?"

"How about because he appreciates you, and he buys you flowers from Montel's. But how did he get my address, and how did he know you'd be here yesterday?"

I shrugged. "Good question. He may have heard me when I told Beth about my birthday, even though I didn't see him nearby."

Carl carried in the plate of burgers and looked my way. "Nicki told me you're getting married. Who's the lucky fellow?"

"Very funny. If I do remarry, it certainly won't be to my boss."

"Nicki seems certain," Jenny teased. "Never underestimate the faith of a child."

"Faith or fancy?" I shuddered. "Not going to happen."

We enjoyed our burgers and conversation. After lunch, I hugged Nicki, grabbed my card, and said goodbye. I sat in my car for a few minutes, reread Blake's note, and tried to fill in the blanks. The one I struggled with the most was the last one, "I look forward to . . . together." What was that man trying to say?

I drove home and decided the afternoon weather was too pretty to stay indoors. I changed into my jeans and took a stroll in my neighborhood. A good walk helps me think. That day, one thought dominated my mind—why would Blake Conner send me roses for my birthday?

~

On Monday morning, I was exhausted after a restless night. How should I handle this situation with Blake? What should I say? *He appreciates me?* When did that happen? My thoughts wandered while I got dressed. Maybe I should call in sick. I left for work as usual.

When Blake arrived, he stopped at my desk. "You look different. Did you get a haircut?"

"Yes." *He noticed?* "Thank you for the roses. My granddaughter loved them too. How did you know I'd be at my daughter's house?"

"Beth mentioned it to Chad as he and I were getting ready to meet Friday."

I fiddled with my necklace. "They're gorgeous."

"I'm glad you liked them." He strode into his office.

Tauni waltzed into our suite and stared at me. "Your hair looks okay, I guess. Maybe took a couple of years off, and your makeup's somewhat better. But you still don't stand a chance to win him over. Not with me around."

She wasn't going to get to me. I got roses. I didn't think she got anything. "Nice to see you. How was your weekend?"

"Not important. I need to talk to Blake."

At least she stopped at my desk this time. My desk phone rang. I held up my index finger. "Excuse me, Blake's calling. Hello?"

"Will you go to lunch with me today?"

"Yes, I'm available for lunch today." We set a time

and I hung up. I had a feeling he knew Tauni was at my desk, and he used the invitation to help me out.

Tauni lifted her chin. "You may have won this battle, but I'll win the war." She dashed away without seeing Blake.

What war? I didn't have plans to fight with her. Was she after Blake, my job, or revenge? And why did she think I wanted to fight for him?

I stood and ambled into Blake's office to verify he knew she'd been at my desk. "You covered for me just now, didn't you? You came to my rescue like I did yours last week when Tauni charged into your office?"

He looked at me. "Tauni? What are you talking about?"

"You knew she was at my desk giving me a hard time. That's why you called and asked me to lunch, right? To get rid of her? Because you know why I can't go to lunch with you."

Blake stood. "Wait a minute. You tell me on the phone you'll go to lunch with me, and now you tell me you can't? You're hard to understand. When should I believe you, and when should I not?"

I stepped closer to his desk. "You weren't aware of her harassment?" I shook my head. "I figured you wanted to help me."

"Like you did me? Because you care about me?"

Although I enjoyed his smiles, they affected me in a way I hadn't expected. I glanced away.

"I heard her. You could write her up, too, and turn her over to HR. She shouldn't talk to anyone the way she talks to you." He picked up several file folders from his desk and handed them to me. "You're usually patient and kind to her. I don't know why you don't tell her off more

often."
    Does he not know he's the same way?

Eight

I squirmed and fidgeted for the rest of the morning. When I told Blake, "I protect those I care about," I meant I had his best interests at heart. Nothing more. He was my boss, and I wanted what was best for him. But I hoped his teasing would stop soon.

Around 11:25, Blake came over to my desk. "You know, Tauni will be in the lobby to see if we leave for lunch together. Are you available for a business lunch?"

A sudden queasiness came over me. "You're probably right." Why was I nervous over a business lunch?

When we stepped off the elevator, Tauni stood at the reception desk, chatting with our receptionist. Looked obvious that she was there to see if we left together. She narrowed her eyes when I looked at her.

Blake gently put his hand on my elbow to lead me through the lobby and out the door—a thoughtful gesture.

We crossed the parking lot to his dark blue BMW.

We decided on a nearby Chinese place and talked about the weather on our drive—a safe subject.

Inside, we were escorted to a booth. Normally, I would place my purse next to me on the cushion, but I kept it in my lap. I wanted something to hold onto. The aroma of garlic and ginger made my stomach growl. I took a quick look around the seating area. Several bench cushions had holes in them.

We scanned our menus in silence. I selected my meal choice, looked around the restaurant again, and wished the waitress would hurry. She brought out a couple of plates of food to the booth behind me and then took our order.

Afterward, Blake broke the ice. "This place could use some updates."

"Hopefully the food's good." I bit my lip.

"Whenever I've eaten here, it's been good." His eyes found the artwork on the wall. "Do you know what kind of flowers those are in that picture?"

I followed his gaze. I noticed flowers in the picture but didn't look closely. I was too nervous to focus. "They look like water lilies. They're lovely."

The waitress placed our drinks on the table. "They're lotus flowers, which are common in Chinese culture." We both nodded like we knew that.

We made small talk for several minutes, then I asked about his family. He told me he had a daughter, Allison Porter, grandson, Timmy who was eight, and a son, Andy. He asked about Jenny and Nicki.

After the waitress brought out our food, Blake asked, "Did you grow up in Nashville?"

"No. Indiana and East Tennessee." Not wanting to talk about my childhood and teen years, I stared at my plate.

"What brought your family to Tennessee?"

I stirred my cashew chicken and sighed. "Do you want the short version or the long?"

"Start with the short."

"My parents died when I was ten. My grandparents lived in Tennessee. They took me home to live with them."

"Ten? That must have been tough. How did they die?"

I met Blake's stare, raised my eyebrows, and smiled. "Sounds like you want the long version after all."

He placed his fork on his plate and nodded. "If it's not too difficult of a topic for you, I'd like to hear your story."

Maybe I should tell him. Especially if my pain could help him in some way to deal with his own heartache. I looked down at my food. "My parents went to dinner one night to celebrate their anniversary. They left me with my mom's sister. Two police officers knocked on our front door and said my parents had been in a fatal accident." My chest tightened. "My aunt didn't want me. I spent four years with my dad's parents in Tennessee until my grandfather died." I kept my head bowed. "Then I moved back to Indiana to live with my aunt—who still didn't want me—until I graduated from high school." I glanced up at Blake.

"But you returned to Tennessee. How did that happen?"

"After graduation, I left my aunt and moved back to the Chattanooga area to attend college. That's where I met Sam." I placed my fork on my plate, clutched my purse, and stared at my lap.

"I'm sorry you lost your parents so young." He slid his hand across the table. When I looked up, he said, "That must have been a difficult time in your life."

"My parents' deaths devastated me." My chin trembled. "But I was relieved to leave the neighborhood where we lived. I never felt safe there."

The waitress approached our table and asked if we needed anything. After she walked away, I peered at Blake. "Living with my grandparents was wonderful. They owned a farm, and they loved the Lord. I found my faith during that time. But living with Aunt Mary . . ." I fought a lump in my throat. "Although her neighborhood in Indiana didn't have as many hoodlums, she was an abusive alcoholic."

Blake's face contorted. "I had no idea." He shook his head and changed the topic back to our children and grandchildren. He then opened his wallet and pulled out two pictures of his family and handed them to me.

I bit my lip. *This might be more personal than when he sent me roses.* The first picture was of a woman who appeared to be my age. "Cheryl?"

He nodded. "The next picture is Allison, her husband, Jim, and my grandson, Timmy."

I looked at the second picture and compared it to the first. "Cheryl and Allison are gorgeous, and they look so much alike." I smiled. "Timmy's adorable"—handsome like Blake. "What does he call you? Papa, Grandpa, Grandfather?"

"He calls me Grumps."

I raised my eyebrows. "Grumps? Why grumps?"

"I tend to be a little grumpy." Blake offered a slight grin. "Or haven't you noticed?"

I looked down at the pictures again. "Where's your son? Do you have a picture of him too?" I handed the photos back to Blake.

His grin faded. "I don't have his picture with me. If you'll excuse me, I need to use the men's room before we go back to the office."

Odd. He didn't want to talk about his son. Able to relax a little, I took a few more bites of my lunch and glanced again at the colorful pink lotus flowers on the wall.

Blake returned to the table and sat.

My body tensed. I did all I could to keep my hands steady. I peeked at my watch. "Our lunch hour is almost over, and we haven't talked business. Why did you call this meeting?"

"To help my assistant out of a bind, and to let her know I'll be out tomorrow. I plan to spend the day with Timmy. He's out of school for an in-service day." Blake signed the credit card receipt and placed a copy in his wallet. "Ready to head back?"

I nodded, and he helped me with my jacket. He'd been way too nice. Why?

On our drive back to the office, Blake said, "Thanks for going to lunch with me. Don't you think it was a good first lunch date?"

I opened my eyes wide. "Lunch date? Although it wasn't much of a business lunch, I can't go out on a date with you."

"I know." He smiled. "But I think we should do this on a regular basis like Debra and I did."

I stared out the windshield. "Debra's your aunt. That's different."

"It might make our travel to Albuquerque easier on you if we get to know each other a little better before our trip."

"How so?" I peered at Blake.

"You spent the last hour biting your lip and clutching your purse. When we're on the plane, you'll have to leave your purse under the seat for takeoff and landing. And what will your lip look like by the time we arrive in Albuquerque?" He pulled down my sun visor and flipped up the mirror cover. A red lower lip greeted me along with a chuckle from Blake.

I sighed. "If I agree to these lunches, I'll need to have lunch with Wes. He's asked me several times already."

Blake glanced over at me. "Wes Thomas? From IT?"

We stopped at a red light and Blake cut his eyes in my direction. "Today was a business lunch. Employees who didn't know Debra was my aunt didn't think we were dating. Chad takes Beth to lunch a couple of times a month to show his appreciation. It's time I do the same."

The light changed, and we drove the last half mile to the office. Blake parked the car, and I hurried to get out.

Back in the office, Blake asked me to set up a spreadsheet he needed that afternoon for a meeting—a statistical report that included several formulas. He explained what he needed, and I got right to work. When he reviewed it and gave me his approval, he requested I attend the meeting in case anyone asked questions about the data.

The meeting was held in our largest conference room which had entrances from our office suite, the president's office suite, and the main hallway on our floor. These meetings made me nervous. When something went wrong, I got the blame. The room was filled with department managers. I took a seat across from Blake.

Tauni's boss, Neil, from our Insurance Department

made the first comment. "Something's wrong with these numbers. This can't be correct." He checked the formula I used and confirmed.

My stomach churned. Blake stared at me. *Where can I hide?* I held my breath, bit my lip, and waited for him to raise his voice and humiliate me in front of everyone in the room. Even after our lunch, I knew he wouldn't hesitate to lash out at me.

His forehead appeared damp, and his lips were a tight thin line. He looked at Neil and back at me. "I must have given Keedryn the wrong information. We'll fix this and come back with the corrected numbers."

My legs were shaky when I stood and followed him out to my desk. "I'm sorry," I whispered.

"Let's look at the spreadsheet and figure out what happened." His tone had a hint of frustration but no anger.

I sat and he crouched beside me. His spicy cologne tantalized my nose. *Focus, Keedryn. Focus.*

He pointed to the monitor. "Looks like you pulled the amounts from the wrong column."

I stared at the screen and nodded. "I'll fix it and apologize to everyone for my mistake."

He shook his head. "May have been mine. Fix it and let us know when you have the corrected sheet ready." He returned to the conference room.

He didn't blame me. *Thank you, Lord.*

After the meeting, Blake met with Chad and wrapped up his priority tasks to prepare to take the following day off. He called me into his office just before 5:00 p.m.

"Let's sit here at my table. We need to talk." We sat across from one another.

I was thankful he wanted to sit. My legs were still weak. Maybe he was planning to fire me after all. I'd never been fired before.

Blake placed his palm on the table. He looked at me and sighed. Then he lifted his hand, made a fist, and lightly tapped the table four times before he stood. What was wrong with him? Why was this so difficult? He wandered over to the sunset painting, turned around to face me, and sighed again. He rubbed his hands together.

I couldn't deal with this. "You are making me more nervous now than when we went to lunch. If you plan to fire me, get it over with."

"What? Fire you?" He glared at me. "Why would I do that? I want to apologize. I'm having a hard time getting the words out."

I softened my voice. "Apologize?" I tilted my head to the right. "For what? You sounded a little frustrated with me earlier, but you don't owe me an apology."

He sat next to me. "Not just for the spreadsheet fiasco. I'm sorry I cause you anxiety."

"Anxiety?"

"All over your face. You looked terrified—not only today. I believe you were afraid I'd berate you in front of everyone. Again." He peered down at the table. "I've treated you like Tauni does—mean and harassing. You could have reported me."

I wanted to reach over and hug him. *He's sorry. That's Amazing.* "I forgive you."

He stood and started to pace.

What now?

Blake looked at the ceiling and then the floor. He rubbed his chin and stopped pacing, then sat next to me again.

I met his gaze and waited for him to speak.

After a long silence, he said, "I'd like to invite you to join me at my table at Ross's retirement party Friday evening."

"Blake."

"Not a date."

My chest tightened. I peeked at the painting of cattle grazing in the pasture. I couldn't respond. *Why did he ask me?* I clasped my hands together and placed them in my lap. Roses. Lunch. Family pictures. *Now this?*

I looked down at the table. "Were you unable to get anyone else to go with you, so you decided to ask me?"

"What?"

I glanced at him. "I'm confused. Do you need me to take minutes at Ross's retirement party?"

"Minutes? No. I thought it would be nice. We could get to know each other better before we make the trip to Albuquerque."

"But I heard you tell Chad . . ." I bit my lip. "Wouldn't you rather take Tauni?"

"What's up with you and Tauni? You're the one attending the conference with me."

"You did say you should take her up on her offer."

"I said, 'maybe.' I was joking. The expression on your face when she left my office was priceless." His tone was softer. He paused a few seconds before continuing. "You started to say you heard me tell Chad something. What did you hear?"

"Part of a conversation." I picked at my fingernails. "I came out of the file room, and your door was ajar. You were talking about the retirement party."

He rubbed his hand over his face and groaned. "I said what I did to get Chad off my back." He cleared his throat. "I didn't mean any of it. Had I known you were within earshot, I wouldn't have said it."

"Blake. It's after 5:00. I need to go home."

"Wait. Please. I know this is crazy—a weird idea, but what if we started over? Had a do-over."

My eyes got huge. I couldn't open them any wider. "A what?"

"Let's rewind the clock and go back to when you first started here at BCH. Where were we when we first met?"

I tilted my head and scrunched up my nose.

"The lobby. That's where we met." His tone expressed frustration.

I hadn't forgotten. I just didn't respond. I should have gotten my purse and jacket and gone home since it was almost 5:30. But he struggled so much with his apology and then again when he invited me to Ross's party. I didn't want to be rude. But I didn't want to complicate my life either. And Blake was my boss. I needed to guard my heart. But maybe somehow this do-over was a part of God's plan.

I sighed, stood, and followed Blake to the elevator. I had no idea what he was up to, and I was physically and emotionally exhausted.

Inside, he pushed the lobby button. "You're not a good sport about this."

"About what?" I chuckled. "I can't figure out what you're doing."

"We're going to rewind to the first day we saw each other in the lobby to the way I should have greeted you then."

"Oh. That do-over."

Nine

The elevator doors opened to the lobby. Most employees had left for the day, but a few lingered. A colorful abstract painting hung over the reception desk, and several live plants decorated the sitting area.

Blake stopped a few feet in front of the elevator. "You were here." He took a couple of steps back. "I was closer to the elevator. Right here. Is that how you remember it?"

He remembers where we stood? "I believe so."

"What did you say to me?"

He was serious about this. "I smiled and said, 'Good morning.'"

He lifted his hand with his palm facing me. "No, that's all wrong."

"What do you mean? I remember, 'Good morning.'"

He grinned. "You did say that. However, back then you said it with a spark in your eye. The way you just said it sounded like you couldn't care less."

I took a step closer to him and lowered my voice. "What do you mean, a spark?"

"That look you gave me. I've never forgotten the spark. Please say it correctly this time."

I looked at him, frowned, and shook my head.

Couldn't have been an I'd-like-to-get-to-know-you spark because, at that time, Sam had only been gone a year. Must have been a he's-a-good-looking-guy spark. I did remember thinking that. I slightly raised my eyebrows and smiled. "Good morning."

"Good morning. You're our new employee from IT, correct? Keedryn, I believe?"

"You wouldn't have said my name correctly. You had a difficult time remembering it."

"Yes, well." He stuck out his hand to shake mine. "My name is Blake Conner. You may call me Blake."

"What? You're telling me that if we were to do this over, I'd be able to call you Blake from the beginning?" I tried to keep my voice low, but this was too much. He had insisted I call him Mr. Conner for the first three months.

A couple of employees eyed us as they hurried past.

"Yes." Blake pointed to the elevator. "After you."

Was he for real? I stepped closer to the elevator doors.

Blake pushed the button, motioned for me to enter, and followed me in.

We stopped on the fourth floor, and I stayed in the elevator. "You took me to the wrong floor. IT's on three."

He blocked the doors from closing with his arm. "I thought it might be nice for you to see the executive area." He smiled. "Who knows, you may work here with me someday."

I stepped off the elevator and followed him back into his office. He pulled out a chair for me at his conference table and sat next to me.

"That's how I would treat you if you started here

today. You know by now I've messed up plenty. I plan to show you respect like I should have from the beginning. And if I don't treat you properly, I want you to report me to Chad." He shifted in his chair. "Will you please join me at Ross's party?"

I'd already decided to tell him yes. But I didn't want to seem eager, so I paused. "I'll be there to help Beth. I can meet you when my work is done." I stood. "Have a good evening and enjoy your day off tomorrow."

"I'll save you a place at my table."

On my drive home, I couldn't get Blake out of my head. He apologized and asked me to sit with him at the party. And I did enjoy the do-over. But I needed to tame the spark. Back then, did he think I was pursuing him? Was the spark the reason he pushed me away?

~

The following morning around 10:00 a.m., I received a call from our receptionist. She said Blake's daughter wanted to bring something up to leave for him in his office. She asked me to meet Allison at the elevator—our protocol when visitors came to the administrative offices on the fourth floor.

I waited in the hallway outside the elevator.

When the doors slid open, a muffled "Oh" escaped Allison's lips.

Her picture in Blake's wallet didn't come close to her true beauty. Her eyes were a brilliant blue like her dad's, and she had long, wavy light brown hair. She wore designer jeans with a striped pink and white pullover knit top.

We greeted one another and strolled to my office area. Allison paused inside our suite door and didn't seem to be in a hurry to leave something for Blake. I offered her the chair across from my desk and moved to the other side to take a seat.

She pointed to my photos and asked about my family. We chatted for a couple of minutes. "I've heard admirable comments about you from Dad."

"You have?"

"He said you're an exceptional assistant. Even better than Aunt Debra."

I kept my jaw from dropping open. "I'm flattered."

"That's what I wanted to see you about."

"See me? I don't understand. I thought you wanted to leave something for your dad."

"I'll write him a note to tell him I stopped by. I knew he wouldn't be here, but I wanted to meet you alone."

She helped herself to hand lotion on my desk and rubbed her hands together. "You've been tremendous for him. He's changed over the past few months, especially this past week. He's a different person. I think it's because of you."

I wrinkled my brow. "Me? I assure you, Allison. I have no idea why you'd think I've had anything to do with this change. I pray for your dad. I'll give credit to the Lord."

"So do I."

"Let's go sit in your dad's office, shall we? Much nicer and more private than here at my desk." We sat next to each other at the small conference table.

Allison glanced around Blake's office and then at me. "I believe God sent you here. For Dad. I've prayed for the Lord to bring a believer into his life. I think the Lord answered my prayers."

"That's sweet." I paused and squinted. "But you don't know anything about me."

"I know and trust my Great-Aunt Debra. She said the two of you spoke a few times before she left, and she believed you deeply love the Lord."

I nodded. "We did talk at times. I didn't know her well, but I liked her." I wanted to ask Allison about her beliefs but didn't want to get too personal.

"My brother, Andy, and I grew up in church. Dad and Mom would never allow us to miss. Dad put God first. He prayed and spent time in God's Word. He taught Bible studies and Sunday school. When I think of Dad, I think of Joseph in the Bible."

Thank goodness she didn't say Joshua. "Joseph? Why Joseph?"

"Did I say, Joseph? I meant Joshua."

Joshua—a man I would want my husband to model? *If* I wanted a husband.

Allison continued. "Joshua was a strong leader. He had faith in the Lord."

I glanced over to the roses painting and pointed toward it. "Would you tell me about that painting. I love the detail."

"Mom was a gifted artist. Let me show you something." We stood and walked over to get a better view. "See this spot here? She painted it that way. She'd say this rose represents us. Blemished. But God doesn't notice. He'll accept us as we are if we'll come to Him. He'll surround us with His beauty, goodness, and love and wash away our blemishes."

I touched her arm. "Thank you for sharing such a personal story with me."

"Mom kept a beautiful garden filled with many rose varieties. She studied them and became an expert in their care and meanings. She taught each of us, too, so we'd know the correct rose to share with others. Did you know each color means something special?"

Allison spoke with love and respect for her parents. I'd heard Jenny share those same feelings when she's spoken of Sam and me.

"My granddaughter recently told me that the different colors have meanings," I said. "She was so excited when your dad sent me roses for my birthday."

Allison's smile faded and her eyes widened. "Dad sent you roses for your birthday?"

"They were from Montel's, and they were gorgeous."

"Dad hasn't had anything to do with roses since Mom died." Tears formed in her eyes, and her voice became a whisper. "He hired a gardener who cares for them, but Dad no longer goes into the garden."

I pointed to the table, and we both took a seat. "I don't understand what you're trying to say. They weren't from his garden."

"Maybe not, but they're roses. He gave you a part of himself—a part he hasn't shared with anyone the past five years." Allison paused and sniffled. "For Dad, roses represent joy, love, caring, giving, kindness, and sharing—so many beautiful attributes."

I lifted my hand, waved it, and shook my head. "Wait. I'm certain the bouquet didn't mean anything personal or special. I'll probably never see another rose from your dad." I looked at my watch. "I need to get back to work, but I'm happy you stopped by. Maybe we can have lunch together soon. What do you think?"

"I'd love to." Allison glanced down at the table and back at me. "Would you help me pray for the Lord to heal Dad's broken heart and for him to begin to enjoy life again?" Allison took a deep breath. "I love him and want to see him happy. I think you may be the key."

"God is the key. I try to be obedient and do what He asks me to do which already includes praying for your dad."

"May I ask you a personal question?" She cocked her head.

"I may not answer but go ahead." I rubbed my hands together in my lap.

"I know you're widowed. Are you involved with anyone?"

I squirmed. "I'm not interested in pursuing a relationship right now. If I do date, it will be with someone who loves the Lord with all his heart—someone totally sold out to God and His work."

"I understand. Please keep praying for Dad. I believe he'll come back to the Lord soon."

We stood, and Allison hugged me. "What color were the roses he gave you?"

"A beautiful deep pink."

"Gratitude, admiration, and appreciation." She smiled. "I think he'll strike again."

"Strike again?"

"Yes, you may try to convince yourself this is a one-time gift, but I believe you'll receive more roses from Dad."

I took a step back. "Okay?" *That will never happen.*

Allison scribbled a note to Blake. We exchanged phone numbers and said our goodbyes.

What a sweet girl. She thought Blake was different because of me, and the roses were confirmation. I shook my head. *No way.*

Thankfully, I didn't have time to think about it. I

updated a database, created new files, and proofed a letter. Then I decided to call Wes to see when he might be available for lunch.

We chatted about his daughter expecting her first baby. This would be his third grandchild. I almost ended the call, but I swallowed and asked the question. "Is your offer still on for the two of us to have lunch together—as friends?"

"I knew you'd come around. Decided to date again? I'm free tomorrow."

"Wes. Not a date. We're two friends having lunch together."

Ten

Blake arrived Wednesday morning, shortly after I did. He wore a big smile. "Good morning."

I greeted him. "Is that a new sports jacket?"

"Tim needed a new pair of shoes yesterday. While we were at the mall, he helped me pick out the jacket and a new long-sleeve shirt to go with it." Blake pulled off the jacket to reveal a striped button-down shirt.

"Your grandson has good taste. I like the multi-colored blues. They go well with the tan jacket."

"Thank you, ma'am."

I could get used to this new pleasant and personable Blake. "Did you and Timmy have a good day?"

"Yes. However, he informed me he now wants everyone to call him Tim. Timmy's too babyish for him."

Blake disappeared into his office and returned moments later. He'd lost his smile. "I'd like to talk with you. Are you available now?"

I straightened. "Your office?"

He nodded, and I followed him inside. He motioned me to his table and sat next to me. "Allison was here yesterday?"

"Yes, she dropped by. She's a lovely girl. I enjoyed visiting with her."

"What did she want?" He spoke in a short, harsh tone.

Why was he upset again? "She left you a note. Did you read it?"

He frowned and handed it to me. "Says, 'Hi, Dad. I love you.' A little odd. She knew I wouldn't be here. I had her son. She could have told me she loved me when I dropped him off at her house. Don't you think?"

I bit my lower lip. "Why else do you suppose she stopped by?"

He leaned toward me. Too close. "You tell me. Why was she here? Are you two ladies ganging up on me?"

I gave him a questioning look and shook my head. "What are you talking about? She said you spoke highly of me, and she wanted to meet me."

"No ulterior motive?"

"I can't think of any." I blinked hard. "Like what?"

He leaned back and appeared to relax a little. Perhaps he realized he was pushing my patience.

"Like the two of you trying to get me back in church again."

"We did talk a little about our concern for you." I used a soft tone. "But we weren't trying to gang up on you. She cares about you. She wants you to be happy."

"She wants me to get married, serve the Lord, and retire in Hawaii. She'd like to visit me there."

"She mentioned the Lord but not the rest." I tried to sound upbeat. But I was too perturbed.

"Mark my word. She's up to something. Tell me about your conversation."

I let out a long loud breath and looked up at the ceiling. This was ridiculous. I looked at Blake. "A conversation between two women who met for the first time. How much information are two strangers going to share?" I glanced toward the door to gather my thoughts. "Honestly. You have nothing to be concerned about. Are you worried that Allison might share personal family information with me? Or are you afraid I might share something with her? I don't understand."

He stood and mumbled an apology for overreacting as he strode to his desk and sat. "I need to do research today. It could take me all day. Do you think you'll be able to pick up lunch for me later?"

I breathed a sigh of relief that our conversation regarding Allison had ended. "Wes and I are going to Corky's today. I'll bring you back something. What would you like?"

His eyes widened. "You agreed to lunch with Wes?"

I nodded.

"Then you'll be free to go to lunch with me Friday. As friends."

I stood and pushed in my chair. "Friday? We already planned to spend time together at the retirement party. You want to go to lunch too?"

"I don't see why not. Lunch will be the two of us. The party will be noisy, and we won't have much time to talk because you'll need to work."

I wasn't sure about this. But I did want to learn more about his family.

"If I agree to go, will you tell me about your family? Now that I've met Allison, I'd loved to know more about Cheryl and Andy too."

His eyes narrowed, and he stood. "Did my family come up in conversation between you and Allison?" His tone sounded resentful and intense.

My heart raced. "What?"

"Cheryl's death. Andy? I don't want you to talk to Allison about either one of them. Do you understand? She doesn't know what happened. And I don't want her to know. Don't snoop where you have no business to snoop. Forget Friday." He sat, picked up a piece of paper, and stared at it.

That was my cue to leave, but I stayed and hovered over his desk. "You said our lunch Friday would be as friends. Friends talk." My voice wavered. "Please don't get upset with me again. If I've overstepped my bounds. Tell me. Don't shut me out."

He ignored me. Like I wasn't there. I had no reason to stay. On my way out, he said, "Shut my door."

I closed it a little harder than I intended.

Forget Friday? I'd asked Wes to lunch to put an end to the not dating guys I worked with, so I'd be available to meet Blake at the retirement party. Although Blake made it clear this was not a date, I didn't want Wes to think it was when I'd always told him no.

I wasn't all that disappointed about not joining Blake at the retirement party. That would have been awkward. But after the do-over, I'd hoped things would continue to improve between us. I didn't expect him to get upset with me and push me away again. And what did he say about Allison? She didn't know what happened, and he didn't want her to know? That made no sense. She knew her mother died in a car accident.

~

I didn't see Blake for the rest of the morning. By lunchtime, my curiosity and concern got the best of me. I knocked on his door.

"Come in." He sounded annoyed.

I spoke to him from the doorway. "I'm leaving now.

What would you like me to bring you?"

"Nothing. I'm fine."

He wouldn't make eye contact with me. I could see his black monitor. He was staring at a blank screen. I slid into his office and shut the door. I tiptoed over to where he sat. "Are you okay?"

"I said, I'm fine."

I knelt to his right and placed my left hand on his right arm where it rested on the arm of his chair. "Blake. Are you sure you're okay?" I kept my tone soft. "I'd be happy to stay and order lunch in for us."

"No. I want you to leave."

The finality in his voice concerned me. "Do you want me to come back?"

He sighed but didn't look at me. He reached his left hand over to my hand which was still on his arm. Then he glanced at me and back again at his monitor. "Of course, I want you to come back. I want you to leave me alone right now. I'm fine."

His hopeless tone concerned me. He continued to stare straight ahead. My heart hurt for him. I squeezed his arm, pulled my hand away, and stood to leave. "I'm here for you, Blake, if you want to talk."

I looked back at him one more time and pulled his door closed. I grabbed my purse and took the elevator to meet Wes in the lobby. I must have looked like a tear-eyed mess, but I was late and didn't have time to freshen up.

"There you are. I thought I might need to send out a search party." Wes's tone softened. "Are you okay?"

I nodded. "Thanks for asking. I just had a rough morning. It'll get better now. Some food and conversation are just what the doctor ordered."

"Then follow me."

Once outside, he led the way to his truck. "Don't look now. But we're being watched by the EVP."

"Blake?"

"Yep. Do you need help to get in?"

"I think I can manage."

The big tires made the climb up into his truck somewhat cumbersome. I managed to crawl inside. "This is huge. How long have you had it?"

"I bought her last month. She's a dandy, isn't she?"

"Roomy and comfortable too." I leaned forward and peered out the windshield at the hood. "I like the dark metallic color. Blue or gray?

"Stealth gray."

I turned to face Wes. "I'll let you know what I think after the ride." He put on a hat and a large grin. "Nice cowboy hat."

"Not any cowboy hat. This here's a Stetson."

I must have insulted him. "Lovely." I giggled.

"Lovely?"

I needed to say something positive. "I like the dark brown color on you."

Wes backed out, and I glanced up to see Blake staring out his window. What was he thinking? And why did he put his hand on top of mine?

Wes looked over at me. "Okay, little lady. Here we go."

"The ride is pretty smooth for such a big truck."

"Yeah. I kind of like ole Betsy."

"You named your truck Betsy?"

"What? You don't name your vehicles?"

"I name them. Mine is Isabel. And before her, Josephine, Molly, Peggy Sue, and Henrietta graced my garage. But your truck is no Betsy. This is a Fred, Bud, or Ralph. Some big dude's name."

Wes chuckled. He pulled up to the restaurant and parked, then came over to the passenger side to help me out. I was thankful because I didn't feel comfortable jumping down.

The smell of smoked meat and barbeque sauce aroused my senses. We sat in a booth near the back. I ordered their beef brisket platter with coleslaw and green beans.

Wes ordered the pulled pork with fries and baked beans. "Do you want to talk about your morning? I've been told I'm a skilled listener. I don't always follow instructions, but I listen real good."

Wes was funny and kind. He bugged me often about going to lunch, but I was glad he hadn't given up on me.

"I appreciate your offer. Some days are more challenging than others. I'm fine." I studied my surroundings. The tables were covered with green and white checkered tablecloths. A sign posted on the wall read: Songwriters' Night. "Have you ever been here when they have live music?"

"I think they do that on Thursday nights. We should check it out."

Yikes. I didn't mean to go there. Sounded like a date for sure. "Please tell me about your family."

Wes beamed. "My daughter's the youngest. She loves life and is full of zeal and joy. She often sings in her church, teaches a group of young women, and volunteers at the food kitchen. She lives and breathes the Lord." He paused and asked about Jenny before he mentioned his son and two grandsons.

The waitress brought our food to the table. As soon

as she left, Wes offered a prayer.

Nice. "Sounds like you did an outstanding job raising your children."

"Not me. The Lord and their mom get the most credit. We divorced seven years ago."

"I'm sorry."

"She was a good woman. Things didn't work out for us."

Shortly before we finished our lunch, I ordered Blake a sandwich and fries to take back to him and hoped he would appreciate the gesture. I smiled at Wes. "I enjoyed our lunch. I had fun."

"I hope we can do it again real soon."

I liked Wes's company more than Dan's. Wes didn't brag on himself, and he gave the Lord credit for his kids. His down-to-earth and delightful conversation brought joy to my heart. I didn't care for his large truck, though, and his Stetson was too big for his head.

Eleven

Blake wasn't in his office when I got back. I placed the lunch on his desk and worked on recordkeeping. He soon returned. With Tauni.

She made eye contact with me but spoke to Blake. "Thanks for lunch, Blake. I had a wonderful time. I enjoyed our conversation. See you Friday."

He'd disinvited me for Friday and was taking Tauni instead. *How insensitive can a man be?* Blake wouldn't look at me. Tauni gloated.

On her way out, she paused and stuck up her nose. "I think I won this time."

I wouldn't let her see my frustration. Not this time. Not over Blake.

After Tauni left, Blake came out of his office with the to-go container and stood by my desk. "I'd like to explain."

Why should I care? I stared at my monitor. "You don't owe me an explanation. I'm your executive assistant. You may take out whomever you wish, whenever you wish, to wherever you wish."

"You're right. But I didn't plan to hurt you in any way."

I hoped I looked confident and uninjured when I stood and left the office. I darted down the hall to the restroom because I needed to get away from him. *He's impossible. I don't need his friendship. I'm stupid and naïve, and I should know better.* I slumped onto the sofa once again. The glimpse of him being sweet and attentive during the do-over caused me to think that maybe I wasn't the only one with a spark. There must have been some interest on his part. But he canceled our evening together and asked *her*, and she rubbed it in. Blake knew how much she got under my skin. He asked her to lunch out of spite because I talked to Allison.

Beth walked in. "Are you all right?"

"A tough day." I rubbed my temples.

Beth sat next to me and touched my upper arm. "What happened?"

I opened both palms and shrugged. "It started when Allison stopped by yesterday to meet me." I closed my eyes and shook my head. "I can't talk about it now. I need to get back and get my work done. I don't want Blake to get upset with me again. We'll talk soon."

The afternoon seemed longer than normal. I didn't speak to Blake, and he didn't speak to me. We communicated by email until 4:00 p.m., then my desk phone rang.

"Come into my office," Blake said.

"I'll be right there." I stood. *What now?* My insides were in shambles. I didn't want another confrontation. My chest already hurt from anxiety. I knocked and entered.

"Close my door."

I did what I was told. Blake took a seat at the conference table and motioned for me to sit across from him. Expressionless, his eyes peered into mine.

"I need you to promise me . . . what I told you earlier

about Allison, and her not knowing what happened. Don't discuss this with anyone. Cheryl's accident . . ." He looked away.

"Blake. I won't."

He peered at me. "Not a word to anyone. I told you too much. None of what I said is to be repeated. Do I have your word?"

His tone intimidated me. I looked down at the table. "Of course."

He moved to the chair closer to me. "And you haven't already told anyone? Wes? Beth?"

He was so close, but he wasn't going to see me squirm. I looked him in the eye. "No. No one."

"I need to leave now. I trust you'll keep your word." He got up, picked up his cell from his desk, and grabbed his jacket from the hook. Just as he was about to leave, he made eye contact with me. "Do you have something else you want to say to me?"

I shook my head, stood, and followed him out of his office. Trying to calm my nerves, I took a couple of deep breaths and released each slowly. I finished up for the day and drove home. It may have been my worst day so far working with Blake.

~

The rest of the week at the office didn't improve. Blake and I both kept to ourselves. On Friday, I heard him on the phone with Tauni. He told her not to come to his office to meet him. He sounded rather forceful with her. He wanted to meet her in the lobby. At least I wouldn't have to see her gloat again.

I called Allison and left a voicemail message to see if we could get together the next week for lunch. Blake would probably be furious when he found out I tried to meet his daughter. But I didn't see how things could get any worse between us, except for him firing me, which might be a blessing in disguise.

Wes stepped into my office. "I'm going out for Chinese. Would you like me to bring you something?"

I gave him my order, and we decided we'd eat in the conference room when he got back.

I finished up some filing while I waited.

When he returned, we ate and enjoyed a few laughs. Forty-five minutes later, Blake opened the door to the conference room and poked his head in. Without a word, he disappeared.

After lunch, I went to see Beth in her office to ask if she'd gotten any additional help for the party. She'd enlisted the help of two other administrative assistants and told me the party was covered. I thanked her and told her I would not attend because I didn't want to upset Blake even more. She understood.

Around 2:00 p.m., Blake called me into his office. He stood when I walked in. "I need you to run an errand for me. I couldn't get out to get Ross anything for the party tonight. I'd like you to pick up the largest bottle of Jack Daniel's you can find and have it gift wrapped. Here's $50.00. That should cover it."

I tilted my head to the right. "Let me make sure I understand. You want me to go to the store, buy a bottle of Jack Daniel's, and have it gift wrapped for the retirement party tonight."

"That's what I said. The largest bottle you can find."

I paused with my mouth open before I spoke. "I'm waiting for you to tell me you're kidding. That's an odd request, even from you."

"Do I need to ask Tauni?"

"I'm happy to go."

I took his money, grabbed my purse from my desk, and left. *Ask Tauni?* He knew that would aggravate me. And I wasn't comfortable going to a liquor store to buy whiskey. I shouldn't have to. He was nasty and vindictive. *Wait. I don't have to.* He said a bottle of Jack Daniel's. He never said whiskey. I drove to the supermarket and bought the largest bottle of Jack Daniel's barbecue sauce I could find. At home, I found a box that happened to look like a wine box and wrapped it in my finest paper. On my way back to the office, I stopped at Walgreens to buy a bow and a card. I spent $13.00. My labor came to $37.00.

When I returned to our suite, I took the gift and card into Blake's office and placed them on his desk. He looked up from a report he was reviewing.

"I'm glad you thought of the card, but you could have found something manlier. I may need to get something else if I have time when I leave today. At least you tried."

I plodded back to my desk, aggravated again. *At least you tried?* He didn't even offer a thank you. What would he say on Monday? He could fire me, but I didn't think he would.

~

Jenny dropped Nicki off Saturday afternoon. After my granddaughter hugged me, she ran down the hallway while Jenny and I chatted near the front door.

"I shouldn't leave her with you. You're a bad influence." Jenny reached for the doorknob to leave.

"Me? What did I do?"

"She's a little you. The last time she was here, she came home and told me I needed to eat more vegetables and get outside and enjoy the sunshine."

I laughed. "Smart kid."

Jenny stepped out onto my porch. "Please make sure Nicki sees your cat this time. She's concerned about her Nana. She thinks your cat is an imaginary friend." She closed the door behind her.

Nicki ran into my living room and stopped in front of me. "Where does Roxie like to hide?"

"Did you look under my bed and the twin beds in the guest room?"

She took off again.

While she was gone, I prepared a baking pan and gathered supplies to make cookies.

When Nicki joined me, she held a framed photo. "I couldn't find her, but I found this." She handed me a picture of Sam pushing Nicki in a baby swing. "Do you miss my Papa Sam?"

"I sure do. Every day."

"Me too."

"What do you remember about him?"

"That he loved me." She plopped herself on the floor and held the picture to her chest. "Nana, I want you to marry a new Papa."

I sat on the floor next to her. "That's up to God, sweetie. You'll need to say lots of prayers for that to happen."

"I pray every night for my new Papa—that man who sent you roses for your birthday." She jumped up and ran down the hall with the photo. "And I'm praying for a baby sister."

I pulled myself up off the floor. Poor thing. She was going to be heartbroken. After she returned, I asked her, "Are you going to help me bake chocolate chip cookies?"

"I'm ready." She climbed onto a chair and scrambled down again. "Did you wash your hands, Nana? I almost forgot." She laughed and ran to the sink. When she finished, she slid to a halt at the kitchen table where I'd placed the utensils and ingredients.

When we put the cookies in the oven, I asked her to help me with another task.

"What?"

"I think I know how to get Roxie out of her hiding place." I set the timer for ten minutes. "Get a can of cat food from the pantry."

"Yay." She scampered to the pantry and grabbed a can.

After we placed the food in the cat's bowl, I asked Nicki to call the kitty. I demonstrated quietly and asked her to repeat what I said as loudly as she could.

She put her own spin on it. "Here kitty, kitty, kitty. Roxie, come eat your supper." Nicki beamed when Roxie moseyed into the kitchen. "Nana, you really do have a kitty."

96

Twelve

Early October

A beautifully wrapped gift was on my desk when I arrived on Monday morning. A tiny gift card was attached with my name, but I didn't recognize the printing. I opened the package with caution. Inside, I found wadded tissue paper and a small, handwritten note.

"Sometimes beautifully wrapped gifts aren't what we expected them to be, are they?"

True. Blake was a beautifully wrapped package, but inside lived a hurting, bitter man. Somewhere in there was an amazing person trying to come out of hiding. *Is that why I'm still here?*

I picked up the package and strolled into Blake's office. I spoke before he looked up from his desk. "Perhaps what's inside the package doesn't appear to be much at first, or of little worth to some, but boundless worth to others. God often takes the simple things and turns them into great blessings and the broken or blemished and restores them to new life and beauty."

"I was talking about the bottle of Jack Daniel's, and you're talking about what, exactly?"

"There's a lesson in your note, but it didn't make me

think of whiskey. Have you heard of the Japanese art that uses gold to repair broken pottery? They restore the broken pieces to an even more beautiful vessel than the original and bring it new life. God does that for us too."

He squinted. "You're trying to make a point here. But I don't get it."

"I think you do." I nodded.

"Your stunt could have caused me great embarrassment."

I didn't want to argue. "Could have?" I kept my tone soft and casual. "You knew I wouldn't buy alcohol even before you asked."

"You're right. In fact, everyone laughed, including Ross. And his wife thanked me before I left. She told me Ross's brother became an alcoholic after he retired, and she didn't want the stuff in their house."

I took a step toward his door to leave and looked back. "Sounds like a simple bottle of barbecue sauce was a blessing for their family."

I stepped outside his doorway. "Keedryn. My change?"

I turned back to him. "Change? There was no change. What was left over covered my labor."

"Are you trying to rip me off?"

He didn't say it in a mean way, but his frown told me I'd better get my purse.

~

Later that afternoon, I took Blake a letter to sign. He glanced up at me. "What happened Friday night? You told me you'd be at Ross's party to help Beth."

I looked down at him and fidgeted. "You were upset with me. I didn't want to ruin your evening. Beth said she had enough help. And I didn't want to see Tauni gloat again."

"Tauni? She wasn't even there."

I creased my brow. "You didn't invite her to join you?"

"I asked you and only you. Why would you even think I would ask her to the party?" His entire face wrinkled, which wasn't his most attractive look. "Ask two women to the same function? How could I possibly pull that off?"

"But when you said, 'Forget Friday,' you meant lunch and the party?" My hands shook. "She said she'd see you Friday. I thought you'd asked her."

He stood and placed the palm of his hand on the back of his neck and sighed. He looked me in the eye. "I tried to apologize. You cut me off."

"What are you talking about?"

"I'd planned to tell you why Tauni and I went to lunch Wednesday. If you remember, I tried to explain after she and I returned. I was upset when I said, 'Forget Friday.' I wanted to apologize and let you know I still hoped to see you at Ross's party."

"This is all my fault?" I closed my eyes for a moment and asked God for wisdom. "We seem to have trouble communicating."

"You made it clear that you're my executive assistant and nothing more. Let's keep it at that. It makes things easier for both of us."

I opened my mouth to speak. Then closed it. Finally, I said, "We can still be friends. Can't we?"

He shook his head. "Friends? I don't think so. Not now."

He handed me the letter and sat. I trudged back to my desk.

His walls would continue to stand tall. I needed to know how to dig out of this hole I'd dug. I pushed him further away with my words. I desired to know the do-over Blake. Smiles. Kindness. Pleasant. Only a glimpse but such a beautiful picture of the real man.

~

I endured the next two weeks with a heavy heart. Blake and I interacted as little as possible. He rarely made eye contact when he passed my desk. The silence got to me. I started to use earbuds with my phone to listen to worship music. Helped me focus on the Lord and not our crazy work relationship. Blake didn't seem to mind me using the buds, which surprised me.

I didn't see much of Beth during this time. She was either busy or not at her desk when I stopped by. I finally caught her at the copy machine in her office. "Blake and I aren't speaking much. I could use your advice."

"Is this about the bottle of Jack Daniel's or Allison stopping by?"

"Seems like I've caused a lot of trouble lately. But this round started with Allison. And got more complicated with Ross's party."

"Do you want to know what I think?" Beth finished at the copier.

I followed her back to her desk. "Yes."

Beth sat in her chair, and I took a seat across from her and explained the misunderstanding that resulted when Blake told me, "Forget Friday." I leaned toward her. "I was sure he meant forget lunch and the party. I thought he planned to take Tauni."

Beth tilted her head. "What? Why did you think that? Blake came alone. After he found out you weren't there to help, he moped around and left early."

I shrugged. "Moped? Not because I stayed away. He would have had a worse time if I'd attended. He was so upset with me. Why does this have to be so complicated?"

"Tauni happened to stop by that Wednesday when Blake left to grab lunch. He needed to get away from the office. She followed him over to the deli, and during lunch, she was flirty with him."

"Typical Tauni."

"Blake has no interest in her. He tried to let her down gently. He thought of a better match for her—a friend of his named Mitch from the gym he frequents. She seemed a little interested. He took them both to lunch that Friday."

I wrinkled my brow. "How do you know this?"

"Chad. He and Blake talk often. Some things I overhear, and some Chad tells me."

"What else can you tell me?" I scooted to the edge of the chair.

"One more thing." She grinned. "Chad said Blake did it for you."

I stood. "Did what for me?"

"Introduce Tauni and Mitch. If she leaves you alone, it's less drama for him too. That and he hoped he wouldn't need to write her up again. Neil raves about her. He says she's the best assistant the department has ever had. I figured you knew all this."

"I had no idea."

"I don't know why he didn't tell you."

I pursed my lips. "He tried, but I wouldn't listen." I sighed and sat again. "What were you going to say earlier about what you think?"

"I believe you're both fighting a losing battle.

You're fighting each other because you both want the same thing." Beth peeked at her cell phone. "I need to go. Chad needs me downstairs pronto."

I returned to my desk. What did Beth mean when she said Blake and I both wanted the same thing? A good working relationship would be nice. Or was she saying we wanted each other? *No way.* He didn't want anything to do with me. And he was unpredictable and moody—why would I want a relationship with him? That wasn't a part of my life plan, and I refused to believe the Lord would want that either.

~

The next week, things remained strained at the office between Blake and me. Our trip to Albuquerque was a month away. I didn't know how I'd be able to endure four days with him if we couldn't find a way over this wall between us.

On Thursday, I became excited for the conference at Beth's church that started that evening. It would end Saturday morning. I planned to leave early and take Friday off. I looked forward to getting away from the office to spend time with other women who loved the Lord.

Blake was in one of his obnoxious moods, so I prayed for patience when he stopped by my desk. "You plan to be gone tomorrow, but you still need to finish these reports for the board meeting next week." He plopped an unfinished copy of the report on my desk. Pages flew everywhere. "What have you been doing? Maybe you're spending a little too much time with Wes." He inhaled quickly and lowered his head for a moment. When he looked up, he said, "These are rather simple reports. They shouldn't take you this long to complete."

His tone was firm but no longer filled with frustration.

I knew I should keep my mouth shut. *Not today.* I stood and glared at him. "The reports will be finished in time for the board meeting on Tuesday." I narrowed my eyes. "And what right do you have to criticize my time with Wes? Rarely, if ever, have I been late getting back to the office after lunch."

"You're right. I shouldn't have mentioned Wes." His shoulders drooped.

My throat tightened. "If you're not satisfied with my work, maybe it would be best if I looked elsewhere."

He took a couple of steps around my desk toward me. "Why do you do that? Poor little Keedryn. Why do you run from your problems? Where's your strength? The Lord is your strength. He's not a wimp. Neither are you."

I was ready to bring it back around. To take my stand.

His face softened and he reached out to touch my arm, but he must have had second thoughts. He lowered his hand and shook his head. "Don't give up on me," he whispered. "I need you here, K. I don't want you to go anywhere else. You should know that by now."

A tender moment, except for him calling me K again—the same name my aunt called me when I was young. I tried to bite my tongue and hold back my emotions, but frustration burned within me. "I'm not sure I know much of anything anymore when it comes to you." My voice wavered. "The past few weeks, you've ignored me. I'm not sure how much longer I can put up with this." I pointed at him. "With you. When you do talk to me, you scold me like I'm a child. What happened to the do-over, Blake? Respect?" I had trouble getting my words out. "I know I'm at fault here too. But I've tried. I don't know what else to do."

I grabbed my jacket and purse and darted past him to the front of my desk. I turned back to him. "I need to go now. If I stay any longer, I may say something I'll regret. See you Monday. Hope you have a good weekend."

Blake stood there staring at me with his mouth open. He was only aware of his own pain. Mine didn't matter. He peered over my head to the open doorway that led to the hall.

I swung around. *Chad.* "Excuse Me." I bolted out the door and hurried to the elevator.

Once inside, I pushed the first-floor button, and Blake called my name. I could have stopped the doors from closing all the way. But I chose not to. Guilt consumed me. He was my boss. I needed to learn how to control my tongue.

I drove through the parking lot and glanced at the building. Blake charged out the employee door. He appeared to be out of breath. What was he doing? Looking for me? Did he run down the stairs? I turned out onto the road.

Thirteen

On my drive to Beth's church, an accident slowed me down. I inched my way closer to an intersection I could take to bypass most of the traffic. Excited about the conference, I didn't want to be late.

I made my way into the church, and Allison greeted me with a big smile. "I'm sorry I didn't return your call. I still honor my father. When he told me not to contact you, I obeyed." She grinned wider. "But he never said I couldn't talk to you if I ran into you somewhere."

"I understand."

"I don't. What happened? Why's he so upset? He's grumpier than ever."

I shook my head. "We barely talk. He's been upset with me for a few weeks. He didn't like that you came to meet me. Caused a lot of tension between us."

"He should be angry with me then. Why would he be upset with you?"

I looked around to see if I recognized anyone else nearby and glanced back at Allison. "I asked too many personal questions. Then I got upset with him. Things aren't going well with us."

"He hasn't shared much with me. Nothing at all these past few weeks. He rarely sees his grandson. I know he cares about you. He's too prideful to acknowledge it."

"I'm okay." I shook my head. "But I'm struggling to stay on as his assistant."

"Please don't give up on him." She brought her palms together under her chin. "You are the one sent by the Lord. I know it in my heart."

"I'll try to stick around through Thanksgiving. We'll attend a conference together next month in Albuquerque."

Allison tilted her head. "Albuquerque?"

"Yes. I need to see this through. But after the conference, I can't make any promises."

"I'll keep praying." Allison hugged me.

"I'd like to find Beth. Do you see her? I think it's about time to start." I peered toward the main doors of the worship center. "Is that Tauni over there talking with her?"

Allison saw where I pointed. "Let's go say hello."

"You can. But I think I might scare her away. I'll wait a few minutes and go over to talk to Beth after Tauni goes into the worship center."

Allison hurried over and joined them.

Tauni Fisher—in church? *I messed up, Lord. I was supposed to show her Your love and kindness.*

Tauni and Allison moved inside. I rushed over and hugged Beth. "I saw Tauni but thought if she saw me, she might leave. Did you invite her?"

"A member here knows her. They're neighbors."

"I'm glad she's here."

"What happened this afternoon? I passed by your door and it sounded like you and Blake were arguing."

I looked down at the floor. "He got upset because I

didn't have the board reports done. He accused me of spending too much time with Wes. And then, when I talked about resigning, he jumped all over me about finding my strength in the Lord." I made eye contact with Beth. "Can you imagine? *He* preached to *me*." I sighed, glanced at the ceiling, then back at Beth. "Then he told me he needed me to stay. These mixed messages of his drive me crazy."

"Deep breath. I hear drums and a bass guitar. Let's go in and see if we can find Allison. We can all worship together. You'll feel better. Maybe the Lord will speak to your heart by giving you new insight into the situation."

We strolled into the worship center, found seats near Allison, and lifted our voices to the Lord. A calming peace came over me.

The evening session focused on valuing others and putting their interests before our own. The speaker shared how we should strive to be kind, compassionate, and forgive one another.

I needed to spend time in prayer.

~

Friday morning, I awoke with anticipation. I looked forward to the day ahead.

The morning's topic dealt with our thoughts—how they can harden our hearts—and our words. The speaker shared Ephesians 4:29: "Do not let any unwholesome talk come out of your mouths, but only what is helpful for building others up according to their needs, that it may benefit those who listen."

My words have gotten me into trouble more than once. *Yesterday, again, with Blake.*

She encouraged us to come forward to pray. I made

my way to the front of the church. I needed to become more compassionate and speak kinder words.

When I finished praying, Tauni stood nearby, and I slid in next to her. "Have you enjoyed the conference?"

"I have. I'm surprised to see you here though."

"Why?" I held my breath. What if she said I don't act like a Christian?

She chewed her bottom lip. "I wouldn't think you need to be here. I do. I got away from church, but I need to come back."

I touched her arm.

"I struggle too with thoughts and my words. I came forward to ask the Lord to forgive me and help me to be more like Him."

"But I deliberately tried to hurt you. And you were kind to me."

"The Lord in me is the kind one. The times when I wasn't as kind, that was all me. I'm sorry. None of us are perfect. I have plenty of faults. If you hang around with me, it won't take long for you to see them."

Tauni looked past me and then at me. She swallowed and cleared her throat. "I want to ask you to forgive me. I've said and done hateful things to you. I want to ask the Lord to forgive me too. Will you pray with me?" Tears streamed down her face.

I took her hands in mine and we prayed. After our prayer, she hugged and thanked me for being an example of Christ's love to her. *Not me. All You, Lord.*

Tauni followed me to my seat. Allison and Beth both jumped up and hugged her to share in her joy. We sat together while the master of ceremonies read the announcements and highlighted the afternoon session and the final session on Saturday morning.

"Will Keedryn Reynolds please stop by the registration desk," the MC said as she was closing her announcements. "You received a delivery during the morning session."

A delivery? Who knew I'd be here? I didn't think I'd even told Jenny.

The four of us approached the registration table together. Beautiful yellow roses were on display in a white ceramic vase.

Tauni touched my arm. "I'll bet those are from Wes." We all stopped.

Beth and Allison both looked at me with wide eyes. "Wes?" Allison asked.

Tauni chuckled. "They're dating. It would only be normal."

I cringed. "I'm not dating anyone. Wes and I go to lunch a couple of times a week but that's all. We're friends."

Tauni raised a brow. "You may want to break that to him gently." She looked off to her left. "A friend of mine is over there. I'll see y'all later."

The three of us continued toward the registration table. Allison grabbed my arm and looked at the lady behind the table. "She's Keedryn Reynolds. Are those roses for her?"

The lady looked at me. "A gentleman dropped them off and told me these were for a special lady."

Special lady? I didn't want them to be from Wes or Blake.

Allison got in front of me and faced me. She nearly shook me when she placed her hands on my upper arms. Her eyes beamed with excitement. She turned toward the table and grabbed the card from the arrangement.

"They're from Montel's. Look at the handwriting—it's Dad's. I told you he'd send more. Do you know what yellow roses mean?"

I tried to grab the card from Allison's hand. I didn't want a repeat of losing this one too. She pulled it away, holding it over her head while awaiting my answer.

"Friendship."

She giggled. "Not only friendship but joy, warmth, and caring. Did you count how many roses he gave you?"

I began to count and shook my head. "Looks like a dozen."

"Fifteen. He gave you fifteen roses. That means, 'I'm truly sorry.' This is amazing." She handed the card to me. "We'll give you privacy to read the card."

Beth laughed at our antics.

Allison and Beth separated but didn't stray far. I sat on a bench in the lobby. Allison's enthusiasm made me wearier. This was bold for Blake. A public place with lots of people. And he delivered them in person. The print was tiny. I squinted and read.

"I'm truly sorry for not treating you with respect. You are important to me. I need you at BCH. If I haven't already missed the chance, I'd like to work on our friendship. Please be patient with me about personal matters."

Truly sorry? I placed my hand on my chest. He did know about roses and what they meant. How important was I? More than just his assistant? That made no sense. Not given the way he's treated me.

I looked up and saw Beth and Allison. They joined me on the bench—one on each side of me. I shook my head. "I don't know what to make of this. An abundance of mixed messages. One moment he's upset and scolds me, and then he sends flowers and wants to be friends."

I turned toward Allison. "What message is he trying to convey through these roses?"

Allison touched my hand. "I think he's crazy about you."

Beth chimed in. "That's what I tried to tell you last week when you stopped by. You both want the same thing—each other. But you're both stubborn and are fighting it." She took my hand. "Let's pray."

I pulled my hand away. "No. Wait. Friendship is fine." Tears puddled in my eyes. "You're both suggesting a lot more than that. I can't. A relationship is not a part of my plan. And besides, he's not serving the Lord."

Beth took my hand again. "Let's pray and ask God what His plans are. Are you willing to do that?"

"Yes," I whispered.

After their prayer, I thanked them both. We stood to make our way back into the worship center for the next session and asked the lady at the registration table if she would keep my flowers until the lunch break. I looked at Beth and Allison. "Are you planning to sit where we were for the last session?"

They looked at each other and nodded.

"I'll be in soon to join you. I need a few minutes."

They hurried into the session.

I wandered over to a window where I could view a park across the street. The trees were turning beautiful shades of red and yellow. But my focus wasn't the trees. I needed to be alone to think. This conference hit on my areas of weakness—my thoughts and words. And with Tauni being at the conference, I saw the impact I could have on one person. I thought about her and knew God's awesome power and love were at work. *With You Lord, anything is possible—even a friendship with Blake. But a relationship?*

Fourteen

When I arrived home after lunch on Saturday afternoon, I took a seat at the kitchen table to write Blake a thank you text message. "Magnificent roses. Accept apology. Friendship good. Won't pry."

Within a minute, I received a response: "Dinner Friday evening? What friends do."

I shook my head and typed my response: "Repair work relationship first?"

"See you Monday. Time for a business lunch."

Business lunch? I'd wait to respond in person on Monday.

In the evening, I reviewed my notes from the church conference, prayed, and re-read Blake's note included with the roses. If he wasn't so adamant about pushing me away, he might be able to win me over. *Keep pushing, Blake. I have no plans to give you my heart.*

At my desk Monday morning, I peeked at my monthly calendar. We only had a few weeks before our trip to Albuquerque. I still didn't look forward to the trip. Could be awkward. I hoped he was sincere when he said he wanted to work on our friendship. That should make it easier to communicate with each other. To travel to a desert didn't excite me either. How many people lived there? Probably crawling with lizards, snakes, and scorpions.

Blake came into the office and greeted me. "Did you enjoy your conference?"

"Yes. Thank you for approving my taking Friday off so I could attend."

"I'm glad you enjoyed your time away."

Beth walked in and addressed Blake. "Chad wants to see you this morning when you get a chance."

Blake nodded and headed across the hall.

Beth looked at me. "Are you going to tell him about Allison being at the conference?"

I stood. "I'm not sure what to do. I'm afraid he'll get upset again. Allison and I were careful not to say much. We both honored his wishes. But he won't know that."

"But if you don't tell him and he finds out from Allison or Tauni, he'll think you're hiding something."

I nodded. "I agree."

"I'll be praying for you."

Shortly after Beth left, Blake returned and strolled into his office.

My gut churned. I didn't want to say anything to upset him. But he needed to know. I tapped on his door and approached his desk. "The roses were beautiful." My voice shook. "Thank you."

He turned away from his monitor. "You already told me that by text." He gave me his full attention.

I focused on the items on his desk. "I wanted to tell you in person."

"What's up?"

He'd learned to read me well. I looked at him. "Allison was at the conference."

"You saw Allison? My Allison?"

I nodded. "I didn't know she'd be there."

"And you spent time together?"

"We did." Probably best if he led the conversation, and I gave short responses.

He stood, came around to the front corner of his desk, and sat with his arms crossed. He waited in silence. I think he expected me to start rambling like I had in the past. "Is there anything I should know?"

"We spent time together but honored your wishes. Please don't be upset with either of us. We share a common bond. You."

"Fine. But stay away from the topic of Cheryl's accident."

"I will." Thankfully, he didn't get upset with me.

We had a peaceful morning working together on a couple of projects. Miranda from HR came into our suite, and Blake invited her into his office. I didn't know they were meeting. I didn't have anything on his calendar. When I left at noon, he and Miranda were still together.

On Wednesday, Blake asked me to prepare a statistical report which he usually prepared, and I typically reviewed for errors. For this report, I would need to gather information from many sources to compile and arrange the data in a spreadsheet with tables and graphs. I spent all morning and part of the afternoon on it. I reviewed the report twice and gave it to him for his appraisal. He said he would review it and get back with me.

He came out thirty minutes later. "Outstanding. But let's try to do it faster next time."

When he headed back into his office, I shook my head. At least I received a compliment before he hit me with the criticism. That was improvement.

Before I left for the day, he stepped over to my desk. "Are you available for lunch Friday? With Miranda and me. We have something we'd like to talk with you about."

I agreed but was curious. Why would Miranda want to talk with me?

We agreed on J. Alexander's for lunch. Pricy but good. They had the best carrot cake served warm with cream cheese icing.

After we ordered, Miranda got down to business. "Blake tells me you do a marvelous job as his assistant, but he doesn't think you're being challenged enough. He feels you are capable of and perhaps desire more responsibility."

I glanced at Blake. His mouth curved into a smile.

"We've discussed a new position for you. Another promotion. This one will involve you overseeing the administrative staff. You'll fully supervise all temporary support staff under the guidance of HR and oversee all administrative assistants in their training, scheduling, and workloads."

"Bonnie's position?"

"She plans to retire at the end of the year. Before we move ahead with this, we want to make sure it sounds like something you're interested in. You'll have your own administrative assistant, and we'll get a new assistant for Blake."

I peered at him.

Blake frowned at Miranda. "We've talked about this." His tone was firm. "We can share the same assistant. I don't see why we'll each need our own."

Miranda sighed. "We have discussed this, but I don't agree with your thinking. With Keedryn on the second floor in Bonnie's office and you on the fourth, sharing an assistant won't work."

Their irritation with one another made me uncomfortable. I hoped our food would arrive soon. Maybe they would calm down to eat.

Blake took a sip of water. "We talked about Keedryn moving to the corner office in our suite to assist me on higher-level projects. Let's discuss this further." He looked at me and spoke in a calm tone. "What do you think?"

My eyes darted back and forth between them. Thankfully, our food order arrived, giving me a chance to consider my response.

When the waitress walked away, I picked up my fork. "I'm thankful for the opportunity, but I would like time to ponder over this. May I give you an answer next week?"

Miranda gave me a half smile. "There will be a substantial pay increase with the promotion. A bigger one than last time."

"I'd like time to think it through."

"You can have until Monday. We need to move on this quickly. If you're not interested, I'll need to advertise. We'll need plenty of time for Bonnie to train her replacement."

We talked a little about my family, upcoming holidays, and company wellness incentives while we ate our lunch.

When Miranda finished her meal, she excused herself to the ladies' room.

Blake's eyebrows drew together, and he leaned toward me. "I don't understand why you need to mull this over. This is an excellent opportunity for you. You'll do an outstanding job.”

“I appreciate your confidence in me, but my concern is something different. I feel I need to pray about this like I did when I applied for my current position.”

He leaned back. “No problem. And you’ll stay in our office suite unless you prefer to move to the second floor.”

“Miranda sounded adamant about me moving.”

His eyes twinkled. “Maybe so. But I outrank her. Although, I’ll agree with whatever you decide.”

At home that evening, I spent time in prayer and asked the Lord to show me if this was a good move or not. I hadn’t expected anything like this after being promoted four months earlier. I made a list of pros and cons to help me make the decision.

After a restless night, I didn’t feel good about the job. What about the other assistants? They should have an opportunity to apply for this position. Especially Beth.

~

Blake was at his desk when I arrived Monday. He appeared to be busy. I didn’t see coffee on his desk, so I zipped to the break room and brought him back a cup.

He motioned me to the conference table, then he stopped typing and joined me. “Have you made a decision?”

“I’m having a difficult time. I could use your help. I’d like the new challenge. But it’s so soon to make a change.”

His forehead creased, and he gave me a half nod. “What are your main concerns?”

“The other assistants. Might look like I’m getting preferential treatment, which could lead to gossip.” I shifted in my chair to get more comfortable. “Don’t you think it would be better if the position were offered internally? Anyone interested could apply."

"I'll talk to Miranda and ask her. She and I agree you're the one person here who has the drive and knowledge to succeed." He sat back in his chair. "If we advertise internally, you'll apply, won't you?"

"Yes, I'll apply."

Within the hour, Blake called me into his office. He stood at his desk. "Miranda said no. We don't have time to post the job internally with Bonnie's plans to retire so soon." He asked me to sit in the chair opposite his desk while he continued to stand. "And no one else qualifies anyway. If you don't want the position, she'll post it externally—not waste time internally." He sat in his chair. "Who are you concerned about?"

"Beth. She'd be as qualified as I am."

Blake shook his head. "Chad would have a fit. He keeps her too busy."

"I still feel she should have the opportunity. Miranda could at least ask her."

He lifted an eyebrow. "If you don't want the position, say so."

"I'll accept the position if Miranda or you will first offer the position to Beth. If she refuses, I'm in."

"You're a stubborn woman."

"I would rather you think caring and fair."

He chuckled. "Caring, fair, and stubborn."

Most of the week, we worked on Blake's presentation for the Albuquerque conference. He would speak in one of the sessions and present highlights of how we work in the rural communities of Tennessee to offer quality healthcare services. We worked together in PowerPoint. I prepared handouts and gathered various company brochures to have available at our exhibit booth. Our trip was two weeks away and preparations were going well.

I hadn't heard anything about Miranda talking to Beth but thought it would be awkward for me to ask Beth. On Friday, Miranda called me and asked me to come to HR. She offered me a chair, skipped the small talk, and went right to business.

"I'd like you to start to train with Bonnie to understand the job responsibilities. She's out on medical leave now but hopes to return soon."

I nodded.

"Blake prefers that you stay where you are, and both share an assistant." She frowned. "I don't think that's wise, but we'll reevaluate later. I recommend you discuss it with Bonnie when she gets back. Blake said you would make the final decision." She shuffled a few papers on her desk. "I plan to run an internal advertisement for your current position to get you help. You can schedule your own interviews. You know Blake's schedule better than anyone."

"Sounds good."

"I'd like you to strongly consider one potential candidate. She's the chairman of the board's niece."

I planned to ask Miranda about her conversation with Beth. But this new information regarding one of the admin assistants being the chairman's niece surprised me.

I shrugged. "Who?"

"Alicia Murray. She's qualified and will benefit greatly by working under someone with your experience. Your choice. But I hope you'll strongly consider her."

My eyes widened. "She's worked part-time in an

entry-level position. If we have other internal applicants, they'll have much more experience."

Miranda's mouth dropped open.

I couldn't believe she'd even suggest Alicia. "I'll think this over. We may experience unwanted drama if we bring her in."

"Don't forget. She's Walt Watson's niece. He'll expect us to make the right decision. No pressure. But I'd be careful if I were you."

"Please let me know who applies." I squirmed under her glare. "Blake and I will discuss and interview them. I'll expect to hear from Bonnie when she gets back to go over my new responsibilities."

I returned to my desk. *Be careful?* I didn't feel good about accepting this position. Something bothered me. Plus, Miranda was Bonnie's boss. I didn't think I wanted her to be mine.

~

On Saturday morning, someone knocked on my front door. Montel's delivered a dozen light pink roses. I looked up the color meaning before I opened the card—admiration and happiness.

I tore open the envelope. "Congratulations on your soon-to-be promotion. I admire you and your willingness to get the job done well. I am delighted you are a part of BCH. Your graciousness and gentleness with me are appreciated."

Must be God at work. I hadn't realized I'd shown grace or gentleness.

I sent Blake a text. "Beautiful roses. Thanks for believing in me."

In less than two weeks, we'd travel to New Mexico together. Although he was easier to work with than before, and we were getting along better, I was still a little nervous.

Fifteen

Monday at 9:00 a.m., I received a call from Wes. We made plans to get together for lunch. Up to now, except for one snide remark, Blake hadn't seemed to realize that Wes and I continued to have lunch on a regular basis. But while we were still on the phone, Blake came out of his office to make a copy. He must have overheard me confirm my lunch plans with Wes.

Blake peered at me from the copier. "Are you and Wes getting serious?"

"Serious? About what?"

He squinted. "Are you getting serious about each other?"

I stood and dashed over to him. If anyone was in the hallway, I didn't want them to hear our conversation. "We talk about our families and things. We're friends. Nothing more."

He fiddled with the settings on the copier and made another copy.

I sensed he wanted to say more, but he hesitated for some reason. Was he concerned about Wes and me? "Can I help you with that copy?"

"I'm good."

He finished at the copier and took a step toward his

office, stopped, and faced me.

"Have I shown you more respect lately?"

I nodded.

"Has our professional work relationship improved?"

"Much improved."

He glanced at the copier and back at me. "Are you ready to start our friendship?"

I wasn't sure how to respond. He continued. "We could try lunch together. Like you and Wes." He took a step closer. "I'll try not to get upset and cancel like I did several weeks ago."

My heart raced. I wasn't ready. I didn't want this trip together to become something more than an assistant traveling with her boss. I looked over to the hallway door and back at Blake. "We'll spend a lot of time together on our trip soon. Let's see how that goes. We may think that's enough friend time."

He appeared to be okay with my suggestion. He shifted his weight to the opposite leg. "Do me a favor." He looked over the top of my head and avoided my eyes. "If it looks like you and Wes are getting serious, tell me."

I blinked. "Sure."

He hadn't hinted to be the least bit interested in spending time with me for the past couple of weeks. But he was concerned about Wes and me. I supposed he honored my request to work on our professional relationship first. He'd done well—been pleasant and patient. I enjoyed coming to the office each day, and I found pleasure in his smiles too.

~

Tuesday morning during break, Beth and I met and strolled around the pond.

"How are you and Blake getting along? Beth asked.

I smiled. "Very well. Since the church conference, he's been easier to work with—thoughtful, respectful, and more interested in my opinions. I've enjoyed working with him."

"I know the two of you experienced some difficult days early on. But have you ever felt, or do you feel that Blake uses his authority to manipulate you in any way?"

"Is that a Beth question or a Chad question?"

She sighed. "Both, but I'll keep everything confidential if you ask me to."

I glanced behind me to make sure no one was walking close by. "In the early months, I was concerned about my job because Blake didn't seem happy with my work. Sometimes, I'd come to the office wondering if I'd still have a job at the end of the day."

"I remember."

"But for the past six weeks, I haven't worried about my job. I feel that his past behavior, when he treated me so poorly, was due to his personal struggles. Whether I remind him of Cheryl or he's still grieving her death, I'm not certain. But I'm seeing the true Blake more and more, and I like what I see."

"Are you at all concerned he may treat you improperly when the two of you are alone in Albuquerque?"

"I'm still a little nervous about the trip, but I'm not concerned that he may take advantage of me if that's what you're asking. Nothing will happen that I don't allow to happen." I lowered my voice. "Meaning—if he's as crazy about me as you and Allison believe, then I plan to guard my heart. He's still not where God wants him, and he's still my boss."

On our way back to the building, we talked about

inviting Tauni to lunch to check in with her since the women's conference. I rarely saw her because she stopped bringing things to Blake. Beth suggested we also invite Allison.

"Would you contact Allison?" I said. "I'll invite Tauni."

Both ladies agreed to join us at Panera on Wednesday. Waiting in line with all those pastries and cookies tempted us, which wasn't a good thing since we were trying to avoid that type of food. We placed our orders and found a table. In addition to our lunches, Beth surrendered to a brownie and Allison ordered a pecan braid. I hoped they'd share.

Chilly wet weather, upcoming holidays, and the conference we had all enjoyed were our main topics of discussion. I looked at Tauni. "Where have you been? You don't come to Administration anymore."

She blushed. "I'm too embarrassed. I know I need to apologize to Blake, but I can't bring myself to do it."

"You could try this. The next time you have something for him, I'll let you take it in, and then you can talk to him like you're talking to us." I folded my hands and placed them on the table. "I'll let you know his reaction after you leave. I'm sure he'll say something. Then maybe you can save the apology for a later time."

Tauni liked the idea. Beth agreed.

After we picked up our food at the counter, Tauni offered to pray. She thanked the Lord for our meal and her new friends.

The four of us chatted and enjoyed our lunch together. When we finished our meal, Tauni asked me, "Are you looking forward to attending the conference in Albuquerque with Blake?"

Allison's face lit up. "I'm curious to hear your answer too."

"I'm not dreading it like I did in the beginning." I glanced at Tauni. "I almost caved and offered the trip to you. But as his assistant, I need to go."

"I would have gone. But he'll be much happier with you by his side." She grinned. "He's interested. He's never looked at me the way he does you. He looks at you with admiration."

Allison and Beth nodded.

I was trapped. Three against one. Four, if I included Nicki's infatuation with a man she'd never met. "Y'all are crazy. You know that don't you? He's been a perfect gentleman. I've seen no hint of interest on his part since the yellow roses."

"Maybe you're not paying attention." Beth took a bite of her brownie.

Allison spoke up. "He's probably concerned about Wes. I think you should stop the lunches."

"Did you tell Wes about your interest in Blake?" Tauni looked at me with raised eyebrows.

I frowned and stood. "I think we need to get back to the office."

~

The Monday before our trip, Blake seemed nervous.

At 11:00 a.m., he called me at my desk. "My PowerPoint is ready for your final review. I revised a couple of the slides, but I'm not sure I improved them. Let me know what you think. I may need to make a couple of changes. Please ask Beth to review them too. Another opinion won't hurt."

What was up with him? He'd never sounded unsure of his work before. I knew he didn't make these presentations often, but I was sure he knew what he was doing.

The PowerPoint was perfect. I sent it over to Beth for her opinion, and she agreed. Neither of us felt changes or corrections were needed.

I ventured into his office. "Everything looks fine." I spoke in a soft tone. "Beth and I both think so. Would you like us to critique your speech? Will that help?"

He scrunched up his face. "My speech? Of course not." He stood and placed his hands behind his back. "I can deliver a speech. I've done this often."

I took a step back. "You seemed concerned about the slides." I tried to sound upbeat. "I thought it might help if you ran through the entire presentation. I'm sure it will be fantastic."

"Sorry. I didn't mean to bark at you."

"Not a problem."

~

Tuesday and Wednesday were about the same. He asked me to review the slides again on both days, but he hadn't made any changes. Then he wanted me to verify the travel arrangements.

Why was he so uptight? Did he always get this nervous when he prepared for a presentation? This was the perfect time to contact Debra.

I placed the call at lunchtime from our conference room on Wednesday. We chatted for a few minutes about her move to Florida and how things were going here at the office. I was guarded in what I said and dwelt on the past few weeks. I then told her why I called. "I need your guidance. Blake will present at a conference on Friday. He's been so nervous. What can I do to help him calm down?"

"Blake's made several presentations. I don't think that would bother him. Tell me more about this conference. What city? Are you traveling with him?"

"The conference is in Albuquerque. I'm attending to run the exhibit booth."

"Honey. You can't calm him down."

"Why is he so uptight?"

"The conference is in Albuquerque, and you're attending with him. I must go now, dear. Blessings."

She wasn't any help at all.

That afternoon, Blake asked if I'd like him to stop by and pick me up the following morning. I agreed. He planned to be at my place at 7:30 a.m.

I packed what I could the night before. Blake told me we would attend a dinner banquet Saturday evening, and I should plan to dress up. He also suggested I bring casual clothes for downtime. From my research on the weather, I prepared for highs in the mid-fifties and lows around thirty. The best part was that I could expect plenty of sunshine. I loved sunshine.

Jenny and Nicki arranged to come to my condo every day to spend time with Roxie and take care of her needs. Although Roxie's not fond of children and hides when the doorbell rings, I hoped Nicki would remember the kitty call and coax Roxie out with food.

Thursday morning, Blake arrived on time. He rang the doorbell and knocked.

He must still be nervous about our trip. I opened the door and invited him inside to help with my luggage.

Blake drove us to the airport—a forty-five-minute drive for a normal person. For him, thirty-three. He weaved in and out of the morning traffic.

My knuckles turned white when I dug my fingers

into the seat. I was a mess by the time we arrived at the airport parking lot, so I struggled to open my door. I just needed to relax and breathe, but I staggered to the trunk. My whole body shook. "May I be added as a driver when we pick up the rental car in Albuquerque? I think I'd like to drive."

Blake pulled luggage out of the trunk and placed it on the ground. "We should be able to add your name on the car." He peered at me and straightened. "Are you okay? You don't look well. You're not getting sick, are you?"

"I'm fine." Our shuttle approached, and I nodded in its direction.

The driver loaded our luggage, and when we boarded, I sat next to Blake. I stared out the window and focused on my breathing to calm my nerves because I wanted my voice to be steady when I spoke. "Was there a reason to drive so fast to get here? I could've been ready at 7:00 if you'd asked me."

"What? You think I drive too fast? Did I make you nervous?"

"More than nervous. I prayed for the Lord to keep me safe for Nicki's sixth birthday. She'll be upset if I can't make it."

He laughed. "I'll try to slow down a bit. When's Nicki's birthday?"

"December 15. I'm taking her, Jenny, and Carl to the Grand Ole Opry. She needs her Nana alive and well for the occasion."

"I'll do my best. I want you around too." He chuckled. "Who'll bring me my coffee every morning if you're gone?"

I shook my head and pursed my lips. *That smile of*

his. He needs to turn it off.

We checked our bags and quickly got through security. We located gate C9 and waited for our 9:20 a.m. flight.

When we boarded, I took the middle seat, and Blake sat on the aisle. Storms in the area caused turbulence on the first leg of our trip to Dallas. Blake asked a couple of times if I was okay. I was until the plane jerked downward a bit too much for me. I reached out for his hand and held tight, which was something normal for me when Sam and I traveled. But Blake? I tried to move my hand, but he put his other hand over the top of mine and grinned. "We'll be fine."

I managed to yank my hand away on the second try. "Sorry."

His eyes twinkled. "I didn't mind."

My face must have been as red as a Nashville Sounds uniform. "I'm . . . I'm . . . fine now." I peered out the window.

Deep within something stirred. A month ago, I thought he might be able to win my heart. *Just now, I think I gave it to him.*

~

Blake seemed oblivious to what happened inside of me and opened his laptop. "You weren't available yesterday afternoon to review my presentation one last time. I sent it to Tauni, and she said it looked fine to her."

"Tauni? Why did you send it to her? I'm sure she did a first-rate job but why not Beth?"

"Are you still jealous of her?" He smirked. "She's dating my friend Mitch and is no problem to you whatsoever."

The flight attendant took our drink order a little later

than normal because of the turbulence.

"In the past Tauni would sabotage me given the chance. I'd hope now she wouldn't stoop so low but not because of Mitch."

"What do you mean? Has she applied for your assistant position?"

"Miranda posted the job first thing this morning. She sent me a text saying three applicants have already responded. Tauni's one of them."

The gentleman next to the window needed to get out to use the restroom. Blake and I moved into the aisle and returned to our seats.

"The others are Terri from Legal and Alicia from Marketing. Alicia will be graduating in a few weeks and is looking for a full-time position."

"I know Tauni doesn't stand a chance. What are your feelings about the other two?"

"Actually, Tauni does have a chance. She recently had a change of heart and asked me to forgive her for being hateful to me."

"I see. The I-want-you-to-promote-me-so-I'll-be-kind-to-you routine."

I raised my eyebrows and shook my head. "The I-asked-the-Lord-to-forgive-me-and-I'm-sorry-for-how-I-treated-you confession."

He chuckled. "And you believed her? I thought you were smarter than that."

"Her commitment remains to be seen, but do I believe she's sincere? Tauni didn't know about my new promotion when she apologized a month ago."

The flight attendant offered us pretzels.

"I'm glad you'll be a part of the interview process," I said. "Your input will be valuable to me. I don't know

Terri well and have had minimal contact with Alicia." I told Blake that Miranda recommended Alicia because she's Chairman Watson's niece. Blake already knew the two were related.

The gentleman in the window seat returned. We moved into the aisle and back again. I buckled my seatbelt. "I'm not sure Alicia's a good choice. I think the full-time applicants would be upset."

Blake received his coffee and handed me my water. "I won't need to be involved. You're capable of making the decision without me. I trust your judgment. Unless you hire Tauni. The other two are fine."

My mouth fell open. "Miranda said you'd help with the interviews."

"Miranda was wrong. I don't get involved in those petty things. I have you to handle them."

Petty? The old Blake had returned. I wanted to fight back but decided to take a softer approach. "Are you saying I do petty stuff? And are you saying you weren't involved in my selection as your executive assistant?"

Blake's eyes widened with a look of confusion.

"You were at my interview."

He fidgeted. "If you remember, I came in at the end of your interview and stayed a few minutes. I wanted to know who could stay calm, cool, and collected with me in the room. Tauni was giddy. Rene from Clinical Services froze. You passed."

"I received the promotion because I held it together with you in the room?" I crossed my arms over my chest. "What about my other question regarding petty stuff? You thought you could avoid that one, didn't you?"

Blake glanced over to the window and pointed. "Oh, look. We're landing. Dallas is bright and sunny today.

Looks inviting."

I raised my eyebrows. "We'll pick up this topic again. Soon. You may want to work on a clever response. I'm interested to know how you're going to get out of this one."

~

Our Dallas layover lasted two hours. Enough time for lunch at Chili's and to arrive at our gate in plenty of time. Blake took a window seat for this part of the trip and said he wanted to rest. I sat next to him in the middle. I think he hoped I'd forget to ask him the "petty" question. A gentleman who looked vaguely familiar took the aisle seat on my right. After he settled in, I looked over at him. "Are you from Nashville?"

"Ma'am, I'm from Little Rock. Been to Nashville several times but never lived there. Is that where you're from?"

I nodded. "You look familiar. I thought maybe I saw you at church or someplace around town."

On the other side of me, Blake mumbled, "Brilliant pick-up line."

I lowered my voice. "Please ignore my traveling companion. He needs a nap and to learn how to behave himself in public."

The man chuckled. "This will be a great line in one of my books."

"Your book? Oh, that's where I know you from. You're Reggie Batson, aren't you?"

"You've read one of my books?"

"I recently read the one about God giving us second chances. I loved the points you made. You've impacted many lives. 'God restores us to full well-being. He delivers us from the pit and offers us the abundant life.'

Your book offers hope and healing to those who have drifted away from God."

He beamed. "So many people need to know the love, acceptance, and forgiveness of God."

"A wonderful reminder to all of us."

I hoped Blake could hear what we were saying. But a soft snore beside me confirmed he hadn't.

Batson and I chatted for several minutes, and then he started to work on another book he was writing. Blake's breathing changed, and his snore grew a little louder. Reminded me of Sam's snore. I grabbed my earbuds, closed my eyes, and listened to worship music for the rest of the trip.

Sixteen

Mid-November
Albuquerque, New Mexico

We arrived in Albuquerque at 3:15 p.m., Mountain Time. The sun shone, and the pilot said the temperature was 40 degrees—a little cooler than I expected. I hoped I'd brought warm enough clothes.

I said goodbye to Mr. Batson and exited the plane. We picked up our luggage and made our way outside to catch a shuttle to take us to the car rental center. I zipped my jacket and looked upward. My mouth fell open.

Blake followed my gaze. "What do you see?"

"The blue sky. I've never seen such a brilliant blue in my life. Amazing." I looked at him.

"I call it desert blue."

In the shuttle, Blake asked, "Have you looked to the east yet?"

"What? The mountains. We're so close to them. They're magnificent."

At the car rental counter, Blake added me as a driver. He drove our Toyota Avalon north and then west to our hotel. I didn't ask to drive. I wanted to see how he did from the airport to the hotel first.

The lobby of the Hotel Albuquerque at Old Town fascinated me. I looked around while Blake checked us in. Overhead, there were three enormous wrought-iron chandeliers suspended from a wooden-beamed ceiling. Wrought-iron candelabra hung on the two walls of the lobby, and dark red, dried chili peppers dangled from each. Native American rugs and Mexican village pictures also lined the walls. Several couches, chairs, and wooden tables offered a place for guests to socialize.

Blake strolled over and handed me a cookie. "Try this. New Mexico's state cookie. The biscochito."

"A state cookie?" I took a bite. Not bad. "May I have another?"

We took our luggage to our rooms on the tenth floor and agreed to meet in the hallway ten minutes later. Blake wanted to check the exhibit area to verify that our supplies arrived and to get set up.

On the elevator back down, he asked, "Is your room okay?"

"Fantastic. Spacious and comfortable. Yours?"

"I've stayed here before and have always found it satisfactory."

"Is there anything truly fascinating to you? My work is petty. The hotel is satisfactory. What has to happen for you to think something is exceptional?"

He grimaced. "I didn't say or mean to imply your work is petty. And you're not if that's what you thought I meant. I appreciate you. In fact, *you're* exceptional. I didn't think before I spoke."

"You redeemed yourself when you said I'm exceptional." We exited the elevator.

"Let's get our exhibit table set up. We'll go for a drive, if you feel safe with me driving, and grab a bite to eat."

"You did better on the drive here from the airport. Still a little too fast, though."

"I'll try to slow down for you."

I hoped so. I needed to slow down my pulse.

We strolled the rest of the way past a mariachi band and the lobby to the exhibit area, then located our booth and supplies. We set up our equipment, display, brochures, and give-away items. Each booth came with two chairs for exhibitors to use.

I added our banner to the table and asked Blake if I needed to always be at the booth. I hoped to attend his presentation. He said he needed me at the booth whenever the exhibit area was open.

"Would you like me to review your presentation one more time?"

"You can check it over in the morning. Let's get something to eat."

The sun had already set, and we drove west. Normally, I don't know what direction I'm traveling, but Blake mentioned the mountains were to the east. We traveled several miles away from them and turned into a strip mall. I scanned the area to find which restaurant he might be taking us to for dinner, but then he pulled back out of the parking lot, and we drove back the direction we came from.

I peered at him. "Did we forget something? It looks like we're going back the way we came."

He grinned. "Look straight ahead."

I stared at the road ahead. Before me, dark mountains were silhouetted in the background and brilliant city lights stretched to the north and south in front of them. "How amazing. I don't think I'd ever tire of this view." The sparkling lights with the mountains looming behind made a spectacular scene.

"You haven't seen anything yet. Wait until tomorrow morning."

I lifted my eyebrows. "The sunrise?"

"A surprise awaits you. If we're lucky, you're in for a treat." His tone sounded cheery. I sensed he enjoyed being my tour guide. "What kind of food would you like? New Mexican?"

"Is that different from Mexican?"

"Sure is. I'll take you to Bienvenido a Casa. Let me know if the food is anything at all like the Mexican restaurants in Nashville."

I tried to pronounce it. "What does it mean?"

"It means 'welcome home' in Spanish."

Blake looked like he knew where he was going. He drove to the restaurant without using a GPS. After he parked the car, he jumped out and opened my door in a flash. He held out his hand to help me out.

He was spoiling me. I glanced at the restaurant. "How many times have you been here?"

"Every time I come to Albuquerque." He opened the door to the restaurant and motioned for me to go in first. "Cheryl was born and raised in Albuquerque." His tone was soft and wistful. "We always made the trip together. This is my first time back since her death." He gently touched my shoulder. "I'm glad you're here with me. I didn't want to come back alone . . ." He got close to my ear and whispered. ". . . or with Tauni."

I looked up at him and raised my eyebrows. "A difficult trip to make alone. But didn't you say it wouldn't matter who came with you?"

His whole face lit up. "Reverse psychology. It got

you here, didn't it?"

I shook my head.

He slid over to the hostess. "Table for two."

So many memories for him in Albuquerque. Might be why he acted so nervous about the trip. That must be what Debra meant when she repeated what I'd said. Albuquerque and . . . you. But why was he nervous about me attending with him?

I took a seat. "Does Cheryl still have family here?"

Blake sat across from me and shook his head. "They all moved to other parts of the country." He perused his menu. "You need to try either the green or red chili."

Of course, he'd change the subject. "Green or red?"

"The chili here in New Mexico is from green chili peppers or red chili peppers."

I opened my eyes wide. "You mean hot peppers?"

He nodded.

"I'm not into hot, spicy foods. I think I'll pass."

"Not an option. You must try one. Ask for it on the side. They'll be insulted if you don't order any at all."

I scrunched up my face. "I don't want to offend anyone."

I looked around the restaurant and tried to determine if there were more Mexican or Native American influences in the décor. I found it fascinating. I loved all the deep, vibrant colors—orange, turquoise, red, blue, green, and brown.

The waiter brought water, chips, and salsa to our table and took our order. Blake asked if Juan was working tonight. The waiter nodded and told Blake he'd ask Juan to come out.

I took a sip of water. "Is Juan a friend?"

Blake nodded. "Cheryl, Juan, and his brother, Luis,

grew up together. They lived on the same street. Juan and Luis's parents died in a small plane crash when the boys were fifteen and seventeen. Cheryl's mom and dad took them in."

"What a gift of love. To take two teen boys and welcome them into their family." Unlike my aunt who only wanted me to support her and her nasty habits.

We chatted while we munched on our chips and salsa until the waiter brought our food. My stuffed chicken sopapilla with grilled bell peppers and onions smelled amazing. I ordered the green chili on the side. I said a quick prayer. When I looked up, Blake stared at me. "What?"

"I'm waiting for you to take a bite."

I mixed some green chili with my chicken sopapilla and took a tiny bite.

"Hot, hot." I gulped down my water. "My mouth is on fire. Do they have sour cream?"

He laughed. "I'll get you some." He motioned for the waiter who quickly obliged and brought me a large serving of sour cream.

Blake's laughter was delightful. I was blessed to hear the joy in his voice several times over the past couple of hours.

A medium-sized man, not quite six feet tall, with short dark hair and a huge smile approached our table. "Blake Conner is that you?"

Blake jumped up. They shared a handshake and a manly hug. The kind with three pats on the back. They chatted about family and the restaurant.

Juan glanced my way. "Who's the lovely lady you've brought into my home?"

"I'd like you to meet my assistant and friend,

Keedryn Reynolds. She runs the office for me."

I stood to shake Juan's hand. He moved in for a hug.

He looked back at Blake. "How long are you two in town? Do you have time to get together to catch up?"

Blake shook his head. "We're here for a conference. We won't have much free time after tonight. How's your brother Luis? Still on the force?"

"He wouldn't do anything else. He's one of APDs finest."

They chatted for another minute. Juan extended an invitation to both of us to stop by again before leaving town. He sounded as though catching up with Blake was a priority, and he'd be happy to meet him anywhere.

After he strode away, I said, "He seems to think highly of you."

Blake nodded. "He's a good guy. His brother too."

~

On Friday morning, I awoke with a smile on my face. *Thank you, Lord, for the wonderful day I had yesterday. I look forward to whatever you have in store for me today.* I'd showered and dressed, but my hair and make-up weren't done when I heard a knock on my door at 6:20. I peeked at Blake through the peephole but hesitated to open the door. Oh well. I eased it open. "I'm afraid you caught me a little too early."

He grinned. "You look . . . natural. Grab your key and come with me. We still have a few minutes."

"Excuse me?" I lifted my eyebrows. "A few minutes for what?"

"Hurry or we'll miss it." His tone expressed impatience.

I was a little perturbed at the edginess in his voice, but I snatched my room key and followed him down the hall. He unlocked his door, grasped my hand, and led me toward the window. I yanked my hand away and darted back to reopen the door that had closed. "If I'm going to be in your room, we need to leave the door propped open. Bring your suitcase over here."

"What do you think I'm going to do? I'm not that kind of guy."

I leaned against the open door and placed my hands on my hips. "I think you're going to bring your luggage over here, or I'm going back down the hall."

He shook his head and grabbed his suitcase. "Yes, ma'am." He placed his luggage in front of the door. "Will you please join me at the window?"

I stepped over to the window and looked to the east. Mountains loomed before me. And a sunrise like no other.

"Incredible. The colors are so, so—"

"Magnificent?"

I nodded. "Amazing. The pink and orange together. What a beautiful color."

"Salmon."

I looked at him and slightly raised my eyebrows. "Salmon? If it were a rose, what would it mean?"

He gave me a look I couldn't quite identify. Possibly a slight smile with a half nod upward. He gazed into my eyes. "Excitement."

"I need to finish getting ready. Breakfast is in fifteen minutes?"

He chuckled. "I'll be over soon."

I hurried to my room to finish my face and hair. *Excitement.* The word itself didn't concern me. The way he looked at me. That smile and nod. His gaze. Could Allison, Beth, and Tauni be right? But this couldn't be

God's plan. *What should I do?*

I worked myself into a tizzy. When he knocked on my door, I almost told him to go away or that I wasn't hungry. Instead, I opened the door.

"Grab your jacket. We're going outside for a few minutes."

"Why?"

"Another surprise."

We hurried outdoors. He offered me his hand, but I shook my head. Sam and I held hands often. I wanted to hold Blake's hand too. But I knew I wasn't ready for where that could lead. Especially with my boss.

He told me to look north this time. Hot air balloons filled the morning sky.

"So many."

"Not that many. Last month they held their annual balloon fiesta here and there were hundreds."

"In Nashville, I've only seen two in the past three years."

"I'll have to bring you back in October next year. The balloons are a sight to behold."

"Is the conference here again next year and during the balloon fiesta?" I stared at his strong profile.

"No conference. I like to plan ahead." He grinned.

I was afraid to ask him what he meant. The balloons held his attention, giving me a good opportunity to study him. "I believe I've found some things you enjoy after all. Albuquerque lights, sunrises, and hot air balloons."

"You forgot the green chili."

We laughed together and strolled inside to the restaurant for breakfast. After we ate, we trekked to the exhibit area to make sure everything was still in order. Blake's presentation was at 10:00 a.m. in the Turquoise

Room. He left me in the exhibit area while he attended the sessions.

I didn't see Blake again until noon when he came into our booth area.

"Why didn't you recheck the slides?" He folded his arms across his chest. "You said you would. They were a mockery. All my hard work and efforts—what a joke. I'll have Tauni fired as soon as we get back."

My jaw dropped open. I forgot to ask him about the slides at breakfast. "What did she do?"

"She changed words, formatting, and pictures. She rearranged the order of the slides and put in those stupid animations."

"I can't believe she'd do such a thing."

"It's not your fault. I don't blame you." His voice calmed. "You mentioned reviewing them a couple of times. I didn't get them to you. I fixed most of the mistakes before the presentation but found a few more while presenting." Blake slumped into a chair. "What did she think she'd gain by doing this?"

A man approached the table for information. After he left, I looked at Blake. "I guess I was wrong about her changing. She probably plans to blame me to make me look incompetent. Apparently, it will help her feel better about not getting my job five months ago." Why did I say that? I shouldn't have spoken so harshly. I rubbed my chin.

He scowled. "She's not going to have a job at all. I'm done with her drama. I hate drama. I'm done with her."

"But what if there's another explanation for the changes." I reached over and touched his arm.

He tried to smile but appeared to dismiss the idea.

"No way we're going to give her a chance in our office as our assistant. I will do whatever I have to. After I share what Tauni did with Miranda, she'll agree with me. Tauni needs to be fired."

"My gut feeling is that Tauni didn't do this on purpose. Something else must have happened." I sat in the chair next to Blake's.

"Like what?" He frowned and shook his head. "You know what I think? You're getting a little too soft when it comes to her. I know you want to believe she's changed. But this is real life. She's still the same Tauni." He crossed his arms.

"Let's give her a chance to explain." I tilted my head and gave him my best pouty look. "Please? I'll talk to her when we get back. There must be more to the story."

"I won't fire her until after you've talked with her. But if she's guilty, she's out. Let's get lunch." His tone softened. "Hopefully, my afternoon will be better than my morning."

We strolled to a nearby café for a quick lunch and returned to the conference hotel. Blake attended a couple of sessions, and I greeted people at the booth. The afternoon whizzed by. Blake suggested dinner and a movie for our evening.

We ended up doing neither.

Seventeen

At 5:00 p.m. with the sun setting, we started our drive to the restaurant. I didn't know where we were going. He said a surprise awaited me. While stopped at a traffic light, Blake blurted out a not-so-nice word followed by, "That's Andy."

Although there wasn't much light, a striking young man who was the spitting image of Blake sat in the car to my right.

"He looks like you. He's adorable."

Thankfully Blake was so preoccupied with seeing Andy that he didn't seem to hear my comment. The light turned green and Blake jerked in behind Andy's car. We took an entrance ramp to I-25 and traveled south. The chase was on. I checked my seatbelt and said a quick prayer. Fear crept in. My voice quaked. "What are you going to do?"

"I'm tailing my son. Don't let that Nissan Sentra out of your sight. I'm going to stay a couple of cars behind, so he doesn't know I'm following."

"Can't you call him and get together while you're here like normal people? Why do we need to break the law and chase him?"

He reached over to me. "Take my hand."

We swerved in and out of rush-hour traffic, making

it easy to tell who taught Andy to drive.

"Are you crazy? Our trip to the airport yesterday morning was a Sunday afternoon drive compared to this." I shrieked. "You scare me to death when you drive with two hands on the wheel. It will be worse if you only use one."

He grimaced. "I didn't know Andy was here in Albuquerque. He left Nashville right after Cheryl's funeral. I haven't seen or heard from him since."

What could I possibly say? My heart ached. "I'm so sorry." My words came out in a whisper.

Concerned as I was, this was not the time to interfere. Blake would do whatever he needed to do to talk to his son. Although, a confrontation with Andy after five years might be a delicate situation. If he wanted to be found, he would have contacted Blake or Allison before now.

I became sick to my stomach and continued to pray. Andy took an exit ramp and pulled up to a gas pump at a convenience store. Blake parked the car and waited until Andy began to fill his tank.

"Stay in the car."

Blake approached Andy slowly, for which I was grateful, and began to speak calmly. Andy said a few words. He stopped pumping gas and quickly jumped into his vehicle. I wrote down his license plate number and shoved it into my purse.

Blake plodded back to our car.

I can't do this again. I jumped out and ran to the driver's side. "Blake. Let me edrive us back to the hotel."

He didn't argue. He climbed into the passenger seat and stared straight ahead.

I set the GPS on my phone to our hotel's address.

"What happened?"

"Not now."

I sighed. "Please?" I asked quietly.

"My son wants nothing to do with me." His voice cracked.

"What if Allison talks to him? Will he listen to her?"

"I don't even know if he lives here or is passing through."

"What about hiring a private detective?"

"He doesn't want to be found." His tone was stern. "Don't say a word. To anyone. Not Allison. No one. Do you understand?"

My gut wrenched. "I understand." I wanted to help, but I didn't know what to do.

I drove us back to the hotel. "Do you want to grab a sandwich here in the hotel?"

"I can't eat. I'm going to my room." We trudged toward the elevator.

"Are you sure you want to be alone? We can sit in the lobby. You don't have to talk. We can just be together." The doors opened and we stepped inside. I looked at him and raised one eyebrow. "I'll hold your hand."

Blake pushed the button to our floor. He smiled, faced me, and brushed his finger along my cheek. "I appreciate your offer. But I won't be good company. You can get room service if you'd like."

"I'm good."

We strolled down the hallway to our rooms. Blake took out his key card and faced me. "I'm sorry I ruined your evening. I'll try to come up with something special for you tomorrow."

I took a step closer and gave him a quick hug. When

I stepped back, I looked up into his eyes. "You didn't ruin my evening. I'll be praying for you and Andy. God is bigger than what happened tonight."

He nodded. "I'm grateful you're here with me."

~

I awoke with thoughts of Blake. The sunrise and hot air balloons. His touch on my cheek in the elevator. I thought for a moment he might kiss me. *Our first kiss. How delightful that would be.*

No, wait. I jumped out of bed and shook myself. *Get that idea right out of your head.* He got upset with me a couple of times. Ordered me to stay in the car. Swore when he saw Andy. Became furious with Tauni. *Think on these things, Keedryn. Stay strong. Dwell on the bad.*

I was surprised by a knock on my door at 6:25.

"I'm not sure I'll be the best company this morning, but I have another amazing view out my window today if you'd like to see it." Blake's tone was dull, and his eyes were puffy.

Did he get any sleep? "I'd love to see another sunrise." I'd looked out my window a few minutes earlier, but the mountains appeared smaller or further away—the sunrise not as grand as the previous morning.

I was thankful his presentation was finished. He'd have a hard time if he still needed to present, especially with all the errors. He offered me his hand and I held it. He led me down the hall and through the door, which was already propped open. The window curtains were closed, and in front of them, a small round table was set for two.

"You ordered room service?"

"The least I could do since you didn't get dinner last night. I'm sorry I let you down."

"Not a problem. You have a lot going on."

"Let me open the curtains and show you the view before we sit." He gave me a half-smile. He let go of my hand and pulled the drapes back to reveal another gorgeous sunrise and snow-covered mountains. His smile grew. "Well?"

"Much better on this side of the hallway," I whispered. "Remarkable."

"And beautiful too."

He wasn't looking at the mountains. I could see him out of the corner of my eye. *What do I do about his attention?* Amid his inner turmoil over Andy, he thought of me when he ordered breakfast, propped open the door, and then offered this view. He stood close. I wasn't ready for his affection, even though I believed he'd almost won my heart.

I motioned to the table. "I think we should eat and get to the exhibit hall."

~

Blake planned to meet me in the exhibit area with lunch at 12:30 p.m., but there was no sign of him. At 1:30, I became uneasy. Did he meet someone else for lunch and forget about me? Or did he leave to search for Andy?

The man in the booth next to mine, Ned, asked if I planned to eat. He was in his mid-fifties—tall and slender with gray hair. I explained my boss said he'd bring me a sandwich, but he hadn't shown up yet. Ned's niece assisted him at the booth. She was a cute twenty-something with a charismatic personality. All smiles. She knew how to engage the attendees. At 2:00, Ned offered to pick up lunch for the three of us. There was still no sign of Blake. I began to worry, which led me to pray for his safety.

I sent texts, called him, and left him voice mail, but no response.

The exhibit area closed at 5:00, and I still hadn't heard from him. The banquet was scheduled to begin at 6:30, so I shut down the booth by myself, sick with worry over Blake. I gathered up our supplies and brochures and threw them into a box.

When I finished with the exhibit booth, I rushed upstairs and knocked on Blake's door. No answer. I zipped down the hall to my room and called him again.

Where are you? I knelt and asked the Lord to protect Blake and for him to find peace over this situation with Andy.

I freshened my makeup and hair, then changed into a long black and white skirt with a lacey white top. I wasn't comfortable going to dinner alone, but I didn't have a choice. I hoped Blake would be there waiting for me.

~

The Alvarado Ballroom overflowed with boisterous, hungry people. I couldn't find Blake anywhere. Round tables were set up for eight guests each.

Ned approached, wearing a dark gray sports coat with black trousers. "Would you like to join Brandi and me at our table?"

"Do you have room to save a place for Blake?"

He nodded. "Have you seen him yet?"

I shook my head. I greeted Brandi when I got to their table. I sat across from her and thanked her for allowing me to join them. She'd changed into a lovely, but low-cut, flower-patterned dress. "You haven't seen Blake by any chance, have you?"

"I have."

Ned looked surprised. "When? Where?"

"I left him in the bar thirty minutes ago. We drank a glass of wine together."

Ned glanced toward the doors. "There he is now."

I followed the direction of his pointed finger. "I'll let him know where we're sitting."

Blake saw me approach and swayed my way. He reached out for a hug. "How's my favorite girl?"

I avoided his arms and stepped back. His breath reeked. "Do you want to go to your room and rest? I'll order you room service."

"No. I want to dance with my gal."

I assumed he meant me. "You can barely walk, and you plan to dance? How many drinks did you have?"

"Only two, babe." He held up three fingers. "A glass of wine with Brandi and then something the dude at the counter recommended."

"The bartender?"

"Yeah, that dude. Bartender. That's a funny name. Do you know him?"

I shook my head. *Focus on the drinking Blake. Not the good version of the man. Remember this Blake so he doesn't break your heart.* "Let me help you to the table."

I took his elbow and led him to a chair. Before I made introductions, I quietly asked Blake for the car keys. I didn't want him to get any ideas about leaving the hotel in his condition. He seemed fine when he gave them to me. Overall, he slurred his words but seemed to think clearly enough. What he said made sense. Until he put his left arm around my shoulder and said, "And this is my girl. She takes care of me. Isn't she breathtaking? I may propose tonight. Shh. Don't tell her. A surprise."

Everyone laughed except me. I wanted to get away from him. Far away. I leaned to my left, and he lowered his arm. If he said anything else causing me embarrassment, I'd kick him in his shin. My muscles tensed, and my heart beat faster. He left me to fend for myself all day and drank his cares away at his own little pity party. With Brandi.

Ned leaned over and whispered in my ear, "I thought the two of you worked together. I didn't realize you're a couple."

I almost snapped at him but calmed myself. "We're not. The alcohol's talking."

"I think the alcohol is telling you what he can't say when he's sober. I think you're more to him than his assistant."

"No. We work together." *I don't want him.*

Apparently, Brandi could hear our conversation or was a fabulous lip reader. She took the opportunity to move to the empty seat on Blake's right.

When a waitress brought salads to the table, I asked her for a cup of coffee for Blake. He glared at me. "I don't want or need coffee. I want a drink."

"Don't you think you've had enough? You love coffee. Enjoy your salad and dinner. We won't be able to dance if you keep drinking." I had no desire to dance with him, but I hoped it would get his mind off having another drink.

He leaned in closer to me. "I'll eat now and drink the coffee. Then I can dance. I promised Brandi I'd dance with her all evening."

My jaw dropped open. I wanted to slap him.

Blake grinned. "She's beautiful, don't you think?"

I glared at him. "Breathtaking."

No one drank while we ate, but I was uncomfortable. Blake ignored me. And Ned spent the rest of dinner talking with another couple who had joined our table.

Dishes were cleared, and the band tuned up. Blake and Brandi stood and strolled arm in arm to the dance floor. My night was over. This evening was a disaster as far as I was concerned. I slipped away to my room. Blake appeared to enjoy Brandi's company and clearly didn't need me interfering. I doubted he noticed or cared that I left.

LUANN K. EDWARDS

Eighteen

Back in my room, I paced. Should I have stayed in the ballroom with Blake? What if he couldn't find his way back to his room? I prayed and let out my frustration. Not only did he leave me to fend for myself all day, but then he planned to dance with Brandi and not me. He'd become an expert at hurting me. *Why am I so troubled? I don't want to care about him this way.*

I changed my clothes and dressed in jeans and a baggy top. I grabbed my phone from my purse to check for messages. A piece of folded paper came out with my cell. Andy's license plate number. I couldn't believe I'd forgotten to tell Blake. I looked up Bienvenido a Casa, placed the call, and asked for Juan.

Seemed like forever before Juan answered.

"This is Keedryn Reynolds. We met Thursday evening. I came to dinner with Blake Conner."

"I remember. Do you need green chili to take back to Tennessee tomorrow?" He chuckled.

"I'm not sure our grocery stores carry enough sour cream to go with green chili. I'm calling about Blake and his son, Andy."

He cleared his throat. "Go ahead."

I related the story of the night before—seeing Andy,

chasing him, and Blake talking to him for a couple of minutes. "But Andy wouldn't have anything to do with Blake."

"I'm aware of all of this." Juan's tone was snippy. "What do you want from me?"

"Did you speak to Blake today?"

"Yes."

"Did he come see you?"

"He did."

"You don't want to talk to me, do you?"

"You should talk to Blake."

"Blake is in no condition to talk. He's drunk. I have new information. I hope you can contact your brother, Luis. Or give me a number where I can reach him."

"We can't help you."

"Can't or won't?" I shook my head. "You don't even know what information I have."

"First of all, Blake doesn't drink. Therefore, I'd say you're lying. Second, Blake gave us Andy's information. Wasn't enough. We couldn't find Andy based on the make and model of the car. What else could you know?"

How dare he call me a liar. "First of all, he drank tonight. He staggered. Slurred his speech. Had stench on his breath. I am not a liar. Second, I have the license plate number of the car." I sucked in a quick breath. "Is that helpful enough?"

"Why didn't Blake give us the plate number?" Juan's tone was softer.

"He doesn't know. I stuffed the paper into my purse, jumped behind the wheel, and found the number ten minutes ago."

"Your story makes sense, except for Blake drinking. That's not like him at all. Give me the number. I'll call

Luis to run a check on the plate. I'll let Blake know what I find."

"I would like you to let me know what you find. Blake is in no condition to understand what we're talking about. I'll tell him in the morning. I hope to speak to Andy before then."

"What? You plan to have a phone chat?"

He must have thought I was an idiot. "Of course not. I'll pay him a visit. Have a heart-to-heart talk. That should be enough." My frustration grew.

"Most likely, he lives where you don't want to go. We have gangs. Drugs. Bad guys." Juan didn't sound impressed with my idea. "You can't go out at night. Blake would have my head."

Gangs? I sensed a tinge of fear and shoved it down. "Then you or Luis can take me."

"Not going to happen."

"What do you propose I do?"

"Give me the plate number. I'll call Luis. He'll run the plate. And tomorrow morning, the three of us will pay Andy a visit." He sighed. "If we can find him."

"You don't think Luis will want to come along?"

"He'll come along, all right. With Blake and me."

"That makes four of us. I'm the one supplying the info. May I have your word?"

"Blake is not going to like this one bit." Juan sighed.

I gave Juan the plate number. We agreed to meet at his restaurant at 8:45 a.m. if Luis was able to locate an address. He agreed to text me before then to confirm.

I sat on the edge of the bed. Although I didn't remember any gangs in my neighborhood growing up, the young men who wore dark hoodies in the alley across from my house always scared me. At age ten, Dad still carried me to the car. Mom covered my ears. I wasn't allowed to play outside. Mom and Dad passed their fear on to me. I shuddered.

I needed to get Blake to his room and set his alarm to make sure he got up on time in the morning.

I didn't take time to change back into my dressy clothes. I'd look out-of-place wearing my jeans in the ballroom, but I didn't care. When I got there, I stood just inside the door. Blake was on the dancefloor with Brandi. She seemed to be supporting him. At the end of the song, they staggered to the table and took seats next to each other. I snuck up behind Blake and whispered in his ear. "Let me get you upstairs. You need your sleep."

"I want to stay here." He looked back at me and shook his head.

"Staying here is not an option. I need you to come with me. *Now.*"

"Go. Away."

I sat in the empty chair on his left. "If you value me as your assistant and want to keep me as such, you will come with me now. If not, then you will need another way to the airport." He glared at me but didn't say a word. "I'm going to my room to gather my things, then check out. I'll return the rental car, then catch the first flight home. My resignation will be on your desk first thing Monday morning." I stood and spun to leave.

A chair squeaked across the floor behind me, and I looked back. Blake stood and got within an inch of my ear. "You can't take back the rental car. There's only one set of keys, and they're in my pocket."

I cocked my head and shook it. "You gave me the keys before dinner."

He reached into his pockets. "On second thought,

I'm not feeling well. I think going to my room is a good idea."

I would have been happier to pack up and leave without him. I gazed up to the ceiling and back. "Take my arm and hold onto me." Without a word to Brandi, we left the ballroom.

In the elevator, Blake decided to act like a child and push all the buttons. I slapped at his hands but was too late. I looked at him and shook my head. "Now we're going to stop on every floor."

When we reached his room, I asked him for his key card. He couldn't produce one. I searched through his jacket and found the card in an inner pocket.

He reached out and touched my arm. "Have I told you how much I appreciate you?"

I stepped back. Apparently, he wanted to talk. Better to speak in the hallway than in his room. "You sent me roses to show your appreciation."

"Roses? If I sent you roses, you must be special." He leaned his shoulder against the wall. "Have I told you how much I love you?"

I closed my eyes for a couple of seconds. His declaration didn't totally surprise me, but I'd expected a romantic setting. Not standing in the hallway of a hotel with him drunk.

Still peeved, I said, "I think the alcohol's talking. Tell me again sometime when you haven't been drinking."

"If I remember."

If he remembered? I shook my head and turned to unlock the door. Blake moved closer. I could smell the alcohol. Nasty.

I turned toward him and put my hand on his chest to

get him to back up. "Stay put."

He belched and steadied himself with his back against the wall.

Nausea overcame me, and I gagged. "I need some air."

Blake slumped to the floor.

Already frustrated, I knew I couldn't get him up. I dropped his key card on the floor next to him. "Get yourself inside." I dashed down the hall.

Getting upset with him didn't show grace and gentleness. But his breath and drunkenness disgusted me. Reminded me of Aunt Mary. Nothing good in those memories.

In my room, I paced for several minutes and held my forehead while I tried to sort through my thoughts. What should I do now? I thought there was something growing between us, then he pulled a stunt like this—ran to Brandi and got drunk.

After my pity party, I checked on Blake. I still needed to tell him we needed to leave in the morning by 8:30.

He sat outside his room door with his back against the wall, looking like a defeated little boy. His key card was still on the floor next to him. He glanced up when I approached and gave me one of his heart-melting smiles. "You came back."

"I want to make sure you get into your room. Try to stand up."

He struggled to get up but sagged back down. "I can't."

I needed help. A hotel staff member, possibly a manager, spotted us. He was a big man. I was sure he could get Blake up without my assistance. "Sir, would you help me get my friend into his room? He drank too much and can't get off the floor."

The employee, whose name badge read Reuben, sat on the floor in front of Blake. "Man, what are you doing on the floor? Do you plan to crawl into your room?"

"Can't get up."

"Don't you know drinking can kill your liver and your relationships? Look at this woman here. What do you see?"

Blake stared up at me. "A beautiful woman."

I knelt next to Reuben.

"First-rate answer, bro. But wrong. Look at her again. She's been crying. Ask her why."

Blake reached out to touch my face.

I flinched.

"Why have you been crying? Your mascara's all over your face."

"I've been praying for you."

"I'm not worth praying for." He looked down at the carpet.

Reuben groaned. "Another wrong answer. If you're not worth her prayers, Jesus died for no reason." My heart leaped. Reuben was a believer. "He died and rose again, so everyone could come to the Father. You know that man?"

Blake shook his head.

Reuben scooted closer to Blake. "What do you mean, no? He wants to give you abundant life, even though things haven't gone according to your plan." He spoke firmly but with conviction and compassion. "He gave up everything for you. That's not enough? He loves you more than any human being could. You need to get right with God. You've known the way and turned your back. He's waiting with open arms to give you a second chance. I'd run to Him if I were you, bro."

Blake's mouth curved slightly. "Second chance? I heard that recently."

Reuben looked at me. "God knows your faithfulness to Him. He wants you to keep doing what you're doing. Don't give up."

He looked back at Blake. "You ready to go inside?"

Blake nodded, and Reuben helped him up.

I stood and unlocked the door, stepped in, and held the door open while the men entered. I told Reuben I'd wait out in the hallway while he helped Blake into bed. Reuben opened the door a few minutes later and asked if I wanted to come inside. He immediately propped the door open with Blake's suitcase. I nodded my approval. I still needed to set Blake's alarm and tell him what time we'd need to meet in the morning. If he'd even remember.

Blake's cell was on the nightstand. I picked it up to set his alarm for 7:00. I told Blake we needed to meet for breakfast at 7:45 to be ready to leave for our appointment at 8:30. He nodded before drifting off to sleep. I turned to thank Reuben for his help, but he was gone.

Before I left Blake's room, I pulled the covers up to his chin, then knelt to say a short prayer. I could hear his soft snore. I asked the Lord to flood Blake's dreams with Reuben's words.

I'm not sure why. Perhaps the reminder of him looking like a little boy in the elevator, pushing buttons to each floor. Or maybe his vulnerability as he waited in the hallway for someone to help. But I kissed him on his cheek. A good-night kiss. Maybe a kiss goodbye. A war raged between my mind and my heart. This was too difficult. *He hurt me deeply today.* I stood and rushed toward the door to leave.

"Thanks for the kiss," Blake said.

I flipped off the light, stepped into the hallway, and listened to the door click shut.

Nineteen

Sunday morning, I still hadn't received a text from Juan. Was Luis able to find an address from the license plate? After I showered and dressed, I picked up my cell to call Blake to make sure his alarm woke him. Before I found his number in my contacts, there was a tap on my door.

Blake didn't ask to come into my room. He stood in the hallway. "Are you ready to go downstairs for breakfast?"

I nodded. "How are you feeling this morning?"

"Other than a headache, I'm fine." He gave me a blank stare.

"Are you packed and ready to check out?"

"Not yet. My alarm blared at 7:00. I remembered I needed to get ready to go with you somewhere. Am I dressed okay for church?"

"Church?"

"Isn't that where you're taking me? God knows that's where I need to be."

"You willingly got ready to go to church with me?"

His mouth twisted to the right. "I wouldn't say willingly. You set my alarm and expected me to be ready. I thought, 'Yes ma'am.' I wasn't about to get into trouble with you again. I remember you saying something last night about resigning if I didn't do what you said." He smiled. "We're not going to church?"

"I'd love to go to church and would especially like you to join me. But not this morning. We don't have time. I think we should pack and check out soon in case our plans take longer than expected."

"Where are we going?"

"I need to finish packing and then we'll talk."

"Hopefully, whatever you're up to will be a notable distraction for me. I'll see you in ten minutes. I'll bring my luggage with me." Blake stepped away from my door.

I sighed. He thought I'd found an activity to do to distract him from his concern about Andy. I hoped our plans wouldn't cause him further pain.

My phone pinged with a text from Juan. "We're on for 8:45. Meet at restaurant."

I had everything packed moments before Blake returned with his luggage. We decided to eat breakfast first and then come back upstairs to grab the suitcases.

We strolled to the elevator. I kept my shoulder bag on my right, next to Blake, and held onto the strap. When we got off the elevator, Blake moved to my left. I moved my purse.

"You don't want to hold my hand?"

So far that morning, I'd kept my emotions in check. But how could I answer his questions without either crying or getting angry and saying hurtful things? I stopped so I could look him in the eye. "You hurt me deeply yesterday." My voice wavered. "I need some time."

The color drained from his face. He gently touched my elbow and led me past the restaurant to a couch in the lobby where we sat next to one another. "I need you to tell me everything that happened last night. But first, I want you to know how sorry I am. I haven't had a drink since college. I guess the alcohol hit me hard. I'm not a drinker." He closed his eyes and shook his head. "Seeing Andy, then losing him for good. I snapped." He leaned forward and stared at the floor.

Part of me wanted to fume. To make sure he knew exactly what he'd done. I couldn't understand why he'd turn to booze and Brandi instead of me. I struggled with that and my own torment over what he'd put me through. But I could sense the anguish in his heart over Andy. And I remembered something from the women's conference. Put others' interests before your own.

I put my hand on his shoulder. "Why don't we check out and find some fast food for breakfast. I'm concerned we're not going to make our meeting on time."

He nodded and stood, then reached out to help me up. I hesitated but grasped his hand long enough to stand. We took the elevator up to get our luggage and returned to the first-floor lobby.

While checking out, I asked, "Is Reuben working now?" I wanted to thank him for helping us the night before.

"Reuben?"

"I think he's one of the managers."

"Sorry, ma'am. We don't have anyone named Reuben who works here."

"But he wore a name badge and a hotel shirt."

"We have a new manager in the Sales Department for the convention side of the hotel. I don't know his name though."

The hotel staffer handed Blake a receipt. "You're all

checked out."

Blake's eyes grew wide. "Could you pull out these bar charges and show them on a separate receipt? I'll need to pay for those with a different credit card."

The staffer frowned but agreed. I tried to look at the bar tab as Blake signed for the charges, but he put his body between me and the receipt.

We loaded the luggage into the car and decided to stop and pick up breakfast burritos.

When we arrived at the restaurant, Blake entered the drive-thru lane. A few cars were in front of us. "I'm puzzled about Reuben," he said. "But I don't remember much."

"Me too. He was odd in a good way."

"I remember he preached to me. He was persistent, wasn't he?"

"He sure was." I nodded.

"Give me time. I think I'll be there soon. Don't give up on me."

We pulled up to the outside menu and Blake ordered two burritos with bacon, egg, cheese, and potato. His with green chili and mine plain. He picked up our food and pulled through to the parking lot. "Where to?"

"Could we park here to eat? But we'll need to leave in fifteen minutes."

Blake looked over at me. "Are you ready to talk about last night?"

"I'd like to start with yesterday at lunch. What happened to you? You worried me."

"I attended the first session and couldn't stop thinking about Andy. To know he's here, and that we leave today . . . I hoped to find him and try to reason with him. I want him home."

I tilted my head. "Even if we find him today, he may not come home. My prayer is that at least the two of you can be reunited and find healing together."

Blake's eyes widened. "What do you mean, 'even if we find him today'?"

I told him about writing down Andy's license plate number after the chase.

"Unbelievable." His face glowed. "This means we may be able to find him through the car he drove. I'll call Luis."

I reached over and touched his arm. "Everything's arranged. We're meeting Luis and Juan at the restaurant. They have the name and address of the car's owner."

Blake's eyes glistened. He opened his mouth and put the car in reverse without saying a word.

I looked over at him. "Please fill in the gaps for me. What time did you meet Juan?"

"We ate lunch together. Luis too. I forgot about bringing you something to eat." He glanced at me and back to the road. "I stayed with them until 2:00. Drove around. Ended up at a bookstore and spent time there. I came back to the hotel and took a nap."

I stared ahead. "Why didn't you answer my calls or texts?"

"I felt lousy. Please try to understand. How would you feel if you hadn't seen Jenny for several years and there she was? But she didn't want anything to do with you."

"I'd feel lousy too." I sighed.

He continued. "I slept until 5:00 p.m., then raced downstairs to help you tear down the exhibit."

"Did you get lost?"

"On the way, I ran into Brandi. She asked me to have

a drink with her. You know the rest better than I do."

I shook my head. This is the part I struggled with. I understood him wanting to visit with Juan and Luis. Even his forgetting my lunch. But going to the bar with her? That I couldn't grasp. "I suppose I do." I looked out the passenger window.

"I messed up. I don't care about her or what she thinks about me. I do care about what you think. Are you okay?"

I couldn't look at him. I shrugged. "A tough day. An even worse evening. I'll be fine."

We pulled into Bienvenido a Casa's parking lot where Juan and Luis waited for us. They climbed out of Luis's car and strutted toward our rental.

"We'll have to finish our conversation later." Blake reached over and gently touched my chin to turn my head toward him. "I need to know what I did that hurt you."

I nodded. When we got out of our car, Blake introduced me to Luis. Luis gave a slight nod and looked at Blake. "She can't go with us. Gangs and bad guys hang out where we're going. The car is registered to a Zoey Jordan. If Andy lives with her, he's in the worst part of town." Luis looked over at me. "It's no place for her."

My heart rate increased.

Blake stepped toward me and spoke so only I could hear. "He's right. Go back to the hotel or wait at the airport. I need you to be safe. I'll join you there as soon as I can."

I looked up with wide eyes. "But I think I can help. Please let me go with you."

"I'd love to have you with me. If not for you, none of us would be going." He touched my arm, and I took a step back. Blake frowned. "But I could never forgive myself if something happened to you. Maybe you can find a church. We could use a lot of prayer. We'll meet up at the airport by 2:00. We'll have plenty of time to catch our flight at 3:30."

I didn't understand why this was happening. I desired for the Lord to use me to bring these two men back together. And I thought visiting this bad neighborhood might help me to deal with any fear that lingered from my past. But I sensed God wanted me to honor Blake's request. I nodded. "I'll see you at the airport."

"I'll fill you in later." He moved closer to hug me but stopped. He brought his arms back down to his sides and whispered in my ear. "I know this is a sacrifice for you. Thank you for not insisting."

I tried to smile and looked up at him. "Remember. Andy's hurting too." I trudged over to the car, got in, prayed for protection of the three men, and asked the Lord to soften Andy's heart.

A knock on my window startled me. Blake motioned for me to open the door. When I did, he reached out his hand. "I've changed my mind. I want your help. I need you with me."

I briefly took his hand, and he led me to the passenger side. "What do Juan and Luis think about this change in plans?"

"Doesn't matter."

"That bad?"

Twenty

Blake raced to the driver's side of our rental car and got in. "I think something amazing is about to happen. I want you to be a part of our reunion. Andy's a great kid." Blake chuckled. "And he's as adorable as his dad." He started the car and followed Luis out of the parking lot.

I scrunched my face. "You did hear what I said."

"I don't miss much. You need to be careful around me. Who knows? You might think I'm napping when I'm wide awake."

I stared at him. Even though I was still troubled by the way he'd hurt me, his smile mesmerized me.

"Ms. Reynolds. You totally ignored my comment."

I blinked a few times. "What? You said something about being adorable."

"After that. I said when you think I'm napping I may not be."

"Like when I kissed you goodnight on the cheek?"

"And when you talked to that author guy on the plane." Blake followed Luis onto I-25 South.

"Reggie Batson? *Second Chances*? You were acting like you were asleep? You heard the whole thing?"

He grinned. "In my computer case, there's a copy of his book. That's the reason I drove to the bookstore before I came back to the hotel yesterday. I got an autographed copy."

"How did that happen?"

"He was at the bookstore. He came to town to speak at a couple of churches and for a book signing."

I twisted and looked in the backseat where Blake had placed his computer case. "May I see your copy?"

"No." He opened his eyes wide and spoke quickly. "He wrote a personal message to me."

"We did his book as a study in our small group at church. If you want, I can get Manuel to review the book with you."

"What I'd like is for you to download some of that music you were listening to on the plane. Reggie and I were rather entertained by you." Blake exited the Interstate and continued to follow Luis.

"What are you talking about?"

"You sang your heart out—oblivious to everything and everyone around you. Not out loud. But mouthing songs. And you displayed such big smiles. At times, tears streamed down your face. I want both kinds of songs— the ones that make you smile and those that make you cry."

"You want my playlist?"

"If you're willing to share. I'll give you my cell later. You can download as many as you like."

I looked upward. *Thank you, Lord.*

Blake stopped along the street behind Juan and Luis in a run-down neighborhood. "Looks like this is the place. We'll get in Luis's car and come up with a plan."

The back of my neck prickled, and my hands became clammy when Blake opened the passenger door.

He cleared his throat. "Are you okay? You look

pale."

The neighborhood was quiet. No sign of gang members. *I can do this.* I nodded and got out of our rental.

We climbed into the back seat of Luis's car.

"Thanks, guys, for allowing me to tag along. I'll be good. I promise." I had no idea what they were thinking, but they seemed gracious enough, considering they didn't want me around.

Blake pointed down the street. "Which place is the Jordan's?"

"The small terracotta stucco apartment on the right a few houses down," Luis said.

"The one with the graffiti covered, white block wall in front?"

"Yep. She's in Apartment C." Luis frowned. "We weren't able to come up with a plan on the drive over. Either of you got anything?"

"I think we send Keedryn to the door and let her break the ice." Blake looked at me.

Took a moment for his comment to register. *Me? Alone? Be strong—don't be afraid. God is with you.* "I think that's exactly what we should do."

"Juan," Luis said. "You go with her. I'll scare the kids. Even when I don't wear my uniform, I'm told I look intimidating."

Luis was built like a linebacker—muscular and thick. If he couldn't join me, I'd be thankful to have Juan as my bodyguard. Would be better than walking down the street alone.

Blake looked at me and nodded. "You've got this. Say whatever the Lord brings to your mind. You're a mom. You know how you'd feel if Jenny were the one who left home." He patted my hand. "Tell Andy I want to talk about everything that happened that day. I'll answer whatever questions he has."

His confidence in me helped to calm my nerves.

~

At 9:30 a.m., we walked down the sidewalk toward the house. I scanned the area. Even with Juan by my side, I felt anxious. What was I doing? If I messed up, Blake may not see his son for the rest of his life. My faith in the Lord kept my legs moving toward the front door.

An older gentleman looked out his front window. Several dogs barked. I saw houses with shutters and shingles falling off. Rusty old cars lined the street. Two with flat tires. Tumbleweed gathered along the walls that separated yards. Although I didn't grow up with tumbleweed back in Indiana, uninvited memories from my old neighborhood, my parent's death, and my abusive aunt hit me hard. I pushed them aside.

We opened a squeaky wrought-iron gate that led to the apartments. The front yard was all sand. A rotting pumpkin sat on the tiny front step of Apartment C.

Juan knocked and looked at me. "It's all yours. I'm here if you need me."

Someone pulled the curtain back on the bar-covered front window. Andy perhaps? I couldn't be sure. A lovely petite young woman with short, purple hair opened the door. I asked if she was Zoey Jordan. She stood a little shorter than me and wore jeans with holes in them. I didn't think they were purchased that way but hard to tell these days.

She whispered. "Who wants to know?"

"My name is Keedryn Reynolds. I'm here as a friend. Do you know Andy Conner?"

"You have the wrong house." She began to close the door.

My voice quivered. Tears sprung to my eyes. I had one chance to get this right. I spoke quickly. "Wait. Please. I see you're expecting. You'll love your child more than you ever thought possible. You probably already do."

Zoey inched the door toward me.

"Imagine not being able to tell her how much you love her."

She stopped the door from closing further.

"Or your son leaving home without ever wanting to see you again—possibly for believing a half-truth."

Zoey looked behind her and then back at me.

"Will you tell Andy that his dad loves him? He'd like to talk to him and explain what happened on the day of his mother's accident. Please."

A man spoke behind Zoey. "Let her in. If she's alone. It's getting cold in here."

Zoey looked behind her. "A guy's with her too."

Juan stepped closer to the door, gave his name, and told them he grew up with Andy's mom.

"I remember you. But for now, only the lady comes inside. Go tell my dad we'll be nice to her."

I turned to Juan. "I'll be fine."

Juan clenched his teeth. "Blake will have my head." Only his lips moved.

"Hush. What does Blake have out there? A machete?"

Juan glanced back to where we parked the cars. I followed his gaze to Blake and Luis who were standing a few houses down. I looked at Juan. "Go." He stepped off the front step and mumbled to himself.

Zoey allowed me to enter. She motioned to the couch and padded to the kitchen which held a small round table and two chairs. The living room was sparsely decorated. In addition to the couch, it contained one old chair, a side table with a lamp, and a TV stand with an older model television. The place had beige-colored tile throughout. The living room was twelve feet by twelve feet at most. I guessed the whole place was less than 400 square feet.

Andy entered the room from the kitchen and sat in the old chair across from me. He did look a lot like Blake, but his eyes were brown. He wore his dark brown hair long and pulled back in a ponytail. I couldn't tell how tall he was but guessed six feet like his dad.

He grinned at me. "Funny. A machete. I think I could like you. What's your name again?"

"Keedryn Reynolds. I work with your dad."

"You came to Albuquerque together to look for me? Are you a private detective?"

"I work with him at Boden Combs. I'm his executive assistant. We're here for an annual healthcare conference."

"Aunt Debra finally retired?" He slapped the arm of his chair.

I nodded. "She moved to Florida."

"How are Allison, Jim, and Timmy?"

"Your sister is becoming a good friend. I haven't met Jim or Timmy yet."

He narrowed his eyes and gave a slight nod. "And my dad? Is he a good friend too? Since you're traveling together, you must be pretty close."

I gaped at him. "I ran the exhibit booth while he presented and attended sessions."

Zoey returned and offered me a glass of water which I gladly accepted. She sat next to me on the sofa.

Andy's mouth curved to the right. "Dad's outside hoping you'll talk me into seeing him, isn't he?"

"He was so excited when he first saw you Friday evening." I looked from Andy to Zoey and back to Andy. "He wants more than anything to work things out with you. He loves and misses you. Will you give him ten minutes?"

"You know the whole story about my mom's car accident?"

"I don't know any of the story except that she died five years ago. Your dad has kept everything else bottled up. That's all anyone knows from what I've been told." I took a sip of water.

Andy stared toward the front window. "I overheard he and Mom arguing before she left the house that afternoon. She said he wasn't committed, and she didn't trust him. She left upset and died in the accident." Andy's voice shook. He looked at me. "I believe Dad's to blame. He was unfaithful to her. She caught him. They argued. Mom drove off distraught and crying and lost control of her car."

Blake was unfaithful? "Stop me if I ask too many personal questions." I placed the glass of water on the side table and clasped my hands together in my lap. "Where did the accident happen?"

"Otter Creek Road in the Radnor Lake area."

"Is that close to your house?"

"A few miles."

When did the accident happen? What time?"

"She left the house around 3:00 on a Wednesday afternoon. The accident occurred about 5:45."

"She must have been at the lake or drove around for a while before the accident since she was gone for almost three hours. Do you think she possibly had time to calm down?"

"Maybe. Some." Andy's eyes narrowed. "Are you sure you're not a private detective?"

I shook my head. "Perhaps she was on her way back home." I glanced toward the front door and back at Andy. "Was your dad on personal leave? I'm just wondering why Blake was home and not at the office."

"He'd been spending more time at home, working from there. When I would stop by, he'd stay for several minutes, then say he was going to the office to take care of a few things. He'd ask me to stick around until he came back."

I squinted and rubbed my chin. "Why would he do that? Why would he work from home? Seems to me he'd spend less time at home if he were unfaithful."

"I hadn't thought about that."

Zoey looked at Andy. "That makes sense. Maybe you should see your dad. Hear him out."

"I don't know." Andy shook his head and spoke to Zoey. "We talked about this Friday night. I'm not sure I'm ready."

"I think you should try." She looked at me. "Andy's tossed and turned the past two nights. Neither of us has gotten much sleep." She looked at Andy. "I will feel a lot better if our child has a grandfather and the rest of your family. Please, Andy."

Andy sighed and nodded.

I stood. "I'll send him a text."

After receiving my text, Blake must have darted to the door. He cautiously entered and shook hands with his son. Andy introduced him to Zoey.

Blake grinned and reached out his hand. "Zoey. Pleasure to meet you."

Zoey's eyes sparkled. She stared at Blake and Andy. "Thank you, Mr. Conner. Nice to meet you too."

"Please call me Blake."

Such a sweet reunion. "That's my cue to leave." I hugged Andy and Zoey. "Hope to see you both again soon."

Andy looked at me. "We'd like you to stay. Dad, she can stay, can't she? You wouldn't be in our house if she hadn't come first."

Blake's forehead wrinkled. "No problem. Stay."

"I appreciate your offer, but I think this should be a family talk." I didn't want to bring Blake any additional discomfort.

Zoey frowned. "Then I should leave too."

"That's not what I meant. You're part of the family. I'm not."

Blake took a step closer to me while he looked at Andy and Zoey. "Keedryn and I will talk about this later. I owe her a great deal in finding you. But I think we should talk first."

I zipped out the door to give them precious time together. The Lord was the victor in this. I expected things to go well. I stepped off the front step. Juan and Luis stood guard outside and greeted me.

Juan said, "How was Andy? Did he seem okay with Blake?"

"I believe so."

We strolled to the car and climbed inside to wait. I sat in the back, relieved to return to the safety of the vehicle, and prayed for Andy to receive the truth.

Luis turned in his seat to see me. "Blake's a good guy. He was good to Cheryl and the kids."

I peered back and forth between the two men. "Do you know the whole story surrounding Cheryl's death?"

Luis twisted his mouth. "We do but—"

I lifted my hand. "I'm not asking you to share anything confidential. Was she ill?"

Juan sighed. "She was ill but didn't want the kids to know. Blake did everything he could."

"Did you ever know him to treat Cheryl in a disrespectful way?"

Juan responded and pointed to Luis and himself. "We were both protective of her. We gave Blake the third degree when they first started dating, and we questioned Cheryl every time they came to visit to make sure he treated her well. From what we saw, he treated her with love and respect. We could see his admiration every time he looked at her and only her." Juan grinned. "Until now."

"Now?"

"We see the same admiration when he looks at you."

I glanced down at my lap. I needed to extinguish this personal conversation.

"How do you feel about Blake? Do you return his affection?"

I frowned. "Affection? Admiration? Have you two been watching Hallmark movies?"

I wasn't ready to hear what they wanted to reveal. I was still dealing with feelings of betrayal. If he cared so much, why did he go off with Brandi? Why not find me?

Luis looked at Juan. "We should tell her."

Juan gave a slight shake of his head. "He may use that machete of his on me." He looked back at me and grinned. "Blake thinks he blew his chance with you." Juan glanced at Luis and back at me.

My heart raced. I didn't want to respond. I stared out the window at the house where Blake was probably explaining to his son the truth about his mother's death. Poor Andy. He carried so much hate all these years. I prayed that the truth would set him free. I peeked at my watch. "Andy gave Blake ten minutes and he's been in there for at least twenty. That's a good sign."

Juan spoke again. "You need to know this before you brush him off. When Blake was in our car he said, 'We may find Andy. That's all I've wanted and hoped for these past five years. But if I lose Keedryn, I'm back where I started. Empty. I need her to be a part of this.'"

I cleared my throat. "Juan. There's more to the story." I bit my lip and sighed. "I don't want to talk about this."

Luis ran his fingers through his hair. "Blake messed up yesterday," he said matter-of-factly. "He knows that. He didn't think he'd ever see his son again. Give him another chance."

"It's sweet that you two care about him so much."

A hooded person in dark clothing ran across the street a couple of houses down. I shrieked and brought my hand to my chest.

Juan and Luis turned toward the windshield.

"What did you see? Did he have a gun?" Luis asked.

The person got into a car parked along the street and pulled away. Luis tore out after him.

I reached up and grabbed Luis by the shoulder. "No. Nothing. He just frightened me. I didn't see anything."

Luis drove around the block and parked the car in the same spot along the curb.

"I'm sorry. I guess I'm a bit jumpy." I leaned back, closed my eyes, and tried to relax.

"Jumpy?" Juan asked. "You looked and sounded frightened. Are you okay?"

I couldn't ignore the tenderness in Juan's voice. Tears welled in my eyes. I told them about the neighborhood where I'd grown up and my parents' death. I looked into two pairs of compassionate eyes. "I thought I'd dealt with all of this years ago. But being here brought back those memories and reminds me of the fear I felt in my old neighborhood." I wiped my eyes.

Juan stretched his hand toward me and prayed. After his prayer, he said, "We know what it's like to lose parents at a young age. You're doing great. You're a tough lady."

My phone pinged. "Blake." I looked up. "Andy's inviting all of us to the house."

Twenty-One

With Juan on one side and Luis the other, we hurried down the sidewalk and into Andy's living room. Blake introduced Juan and Luis. Everyone appeared happy. Andy and Zoey were holding hands and smiling too. I stood near the front door and took in everything.

Andy and Blake stood side by side. I hadn't noticed earlier, but they were dressed similarly. Both wore black jeans and striped shirts. Andy's was more casual and well worn. Each were handsome and shared great smiles. They both wiped their eyes a few times while they talked.

Juan stepped over to me and led me to the front window. "Are you okay?"

I pulled back the curtain and stared out to the street. "I'm fine." I lowered my hand and turned to Juan.

"I'll continue to pray for you." He hugged me and then walked over to Luis.

I glanced at Zoey and Andy. Neither wore a wedding ring. When I was young, I endured ridicule from my aunt because my parents had gotten married after my birth. I hated to think that Andy and Zoey's child might experience that too. *Lord, I pray they seal their love through marriage before their baby is born.*

Zoey came over to me. "I'm amazed at how much Andy resembles his dad. Looks like I know what to expect as he gets older."

"And I know what Blake looked like when he was young."

Blake looked across the room at me and winked, then motioned for me to come closer. "Andy wants to call Allison. It's about 11:15 there. She may still be at church. Could we use your phone? She may pick up sooner thinking something's happened to me."

"You want me to scare her into answering her phone? Nice."

We moved to the kitchen and gathered at the table around my cell. She answered on the fourth ring and whispered into the phone.

"Keedryn? Is everything okay?"

"Everything's fine. Are you someplace where you can hear me well? I have you on speakerphone."

She spoke louder. "I can hear you now. I moved into one of the small classrooms."

"Hi, Allison. This is Juan and Luis Ortiz."

"I wondered if Dad would be able to see you two. I'm so glad you could connect. Is Dad there too?"

Blake stepped in between Juan and me and grabbed my hand. "I'm here. Is everyone okay at home?"

I was uncomfortable but didn't pull my hand away. I didn't want to spoil this family reunion in any way.

"Jim and Tim are fine. Tim misses you. He wants to know when you can take him to a Titans' game."

"Tell him soon."

A single tear dropped down Andy's cheek. "Hi, Allie."

Allison squealed. "Andy?"

Silence.

"Andy is that you?" She whispered. "You're in Albuquerque? Have you been there this whole time?"

"About eighteen months."

She sobbed. "I've missed you so much. I've been so worried about you. Are you okay?"

"I'm good. I live with my girlfriend, Zoey."

"Is she there now?"

Zoey stepped closer to the table. "Hello, Allison."

"Hi. Thanks for looking after my brother. I hope we can meet soon."

Blake smiled. "Zoey's done a great job."

I could hear some background noise through the phone.

"I need to go," Allison said. "People are coming into this room. Andy, give Dad your phone number so I can call you."

"Sure, Sis. Take care. Love you."

"You too, bumblehead. Bye, everyone."

Andy chuckled. "I do miss her pet names for me." He stood across the table from us and nudged Zoey's arm. They both looked over at Blake and me with our hands clasped together. *They'll think I lied.* I pulled my hand away, stepped over to Andy and Zoey, and whispered, "It's complicated."

They both nodded.

"I've always thought that about Dad," Andy said.

We chatted in the kitchen a while longer and suggested that Andy and Zoey come to visit us in Nashville. We exchanged phone numbers, grabbed the two kitchen chairs, and moved to the living room. Andy and Zoey plopped down on the sofa. Juan and Luis sat on the kitchen chairs.

I touched Blake's arm before he sat. "I know you don't want to go," I whispered. "But I think Andy and Zoey need some time to themselves to process all that's happened this morning. They look exhausted."

He frowned and looked at Andy. "We'd better go now. We have a plane to catch in a few hours." He looked at me and mouthed, "We could change our reservations."

I shook my head and shrugged. I needed time to process everything too. "I need to get back. You can do whatever."

His forehead creased. He looked at the couple sitting on the sofa. "Zoey, thank you for your hospitality. I'm glad we got to meet."

Zoey stood. "You're always welcome."

Andy joined her. "Dad. Keedryn. We'll see you again soon."

Blake wiped a tear from his eye. "That's great, son. I love you." He reached out to give Andy a hug.

Andy stepped back and extended his hand. "Thanks, Dad. I'm glad we had this chat."

Blake nodded. "Me too."

We said our good-byes, strolled down the sidewalk, and returned to our cars.

Juan nudged my arm. "You were amazing talking to Zoey and getting her to let you inside. I'm glad Blake listened to us and allowed you to come along. He can be so pig-headed sometimes."

"Why are you taking credit for something that was my idea?" Blake laughed.

I opened the passenger door of our rental and looked at the three men. "Juan. Luis. Thanks for letting me tag along. A pleasure meeting you."

"We love happy endings and we got one today," Juan said. "You're welcome here anytime. Come back and see me at the restaurant. I'll be sure to serve you the best green chili in the city."

"We'll be back," Blake said. "I promised her a trip to the balloon fiesta next year."

Luis stepped closer to me. "A date eleven months in advance?" he whispered. "Sounds like admiration and affection to me." He turned toward Blake. "Looks like we'll be seeing you both next year."

Juan hugged me. "He's expecting his ring to be on your finger," he whispered. "You know that, don't you? Add us to the invite list. We'll be there if possible."

I touched his arm. "Thanks for everything. I'll try your green chili again *if* I return."

We said our goodbyes and drove off. Blake and I were both quiet. I think we each needed time for personal reflection.

Blake cleared his throat. "We could stay longer. I can take the time off. Do you have paid leave available?"

"I need to get back, but you're welcome to stay. Please drop me off at the airport. You can probably keep the car and postpone your flight." I peeked at my cell. "I should be able to do that for you from my phone and reserve a room for you."

He sighed. "Never mind. It's still kind of early for lunch. Starbucks?"

"Chad would understand if you stayed longer. I think it's a great idea."

He shook his head. "So, Starbucks?"

"Sounds good." I cocked my head and studied him. *Why won't he stay?*

He glanced over at me. "You were wonderful today.

Andy and Zoey couldn't say enough good about you after you left. They said you asked some thought-provoking questions about me spending extra time at home. Questions about the accident."

I widened my eyes and brought my hand up to cover my mouth. "I asked Andy about the accident."

Blake chuckled. "Not a problem. I didn't ask you not to talk to Andy. You were my bridge to him—the reason we were able to meet. Those questions you asked paved the way."

"Not me. All God."

"He answered your prayers today."

Blake offered me his hand, but I wasn't ready. He placed his hand back on the steering wheel. "I heard Juan and Luis talk about you getting spooked. What was that about?"

"No big deal." I told Blake about the hooded person and how he'd frightened me.

His voice cracked. "I'm sorry. I never thought about your childhood experiences."

I glanced at Blake. "I'll be okay. I'll contact Manuel when I get home to meet with him. He'll give me wise counsel and pray with me. I've got to get a grip on this attack of fear before it gets worse."

"Did you feel anxiety when you offered to go with us to Andy's house?"

I stared out the windshield. "I did once Luis confirmed that the area of town where Andy lived wasn't safe."

"Then why did you agree to go? I would have understood if you'd told me no."

Why did I feel the need to tag along? "Two reasons. I can't imagine what my life would be like without

Jenny. I knew how important it was for you to have Andy back in yours, and I wanted to share in your reunion." I looked down at my clasped hands in my lap. "I also needed to face my fear."

"You and your faith are an inspiration to many. Me included."

I looked up, and when he glanced at me, the corners of his eyes crinkled. "Not sure how much faith I have. I thought I'd dealt with my childhood and teen years a long time ago." I stared ahead. "Why now with everything else this weekend?"

Blake took a deep breath. "I know you're still upset with me. Please talk to me. What did I do that hurt you?"

He ignored me all day and night, forgot about me and ran to Brandi, and got drunk. If I truly meant something to him like everyone's told me, why didn't his actions show that he cared? I wasn't ready to discuss any of it with him. Truth is, he made me feel unimportant. He couldn't possibly care about me.

"I need you to talk to me . . . Cheryl shut down . . . She got to the point where she held everything inside. Talk. Please."

I didn't want to cause him further anguish, even though he'd caused me plenty. "What should have been a pleasant evening turned into a fiasco."

"Fiasco?"

I scowled. "You were drunk. You had to lean on me to make it upstairs. You behaved like a child in the elevator. You got too chummy outside the doorway to your room, you collapsed on the floor, and your breath was disgusting."

He pulled the car into a bank parking lot and parked. He reached over to touch my arm, but I jerked away. His touch wasn't welcomed.

I glared at him.

His face turned pale. "How chummy?"

"Not *that* chummy. You just got too close."

He let out a long exhale.

I crossed my arms and focused ahead. "Close enough for a gross kiss."

"You think a kiss from me would be gross?"

"At that moment and with your breath, it wouldn't have been anything like the romantic, gentle, first kiss I dreamed about." I jerked my head down. Oh, my. "Tell me I didn't say that out loud."

"You dreamed about our first kiss?" I could hear the pleasure in his voice without seeing his face.

I frowned. "Yesterday morning. I guess after your wanting to hold hands, and with how sweet you'd been to me, I expected a somewhat romantic evening." I could see him staring at me out the corner of my eye.

"You were hoping for romance and I disappointed you."

I glanced at Blake. "Not hoping, necessarily. Just expecting. There's a difference."

He nodded and closed his eyes for a moment. "I'm sorry. How can I make this up to you? There must be something I can do." His tone was compassionate.

I looked out the windshield. "There's no need to make it up to me. I'm fine."

"But I'm sure I can deliver the romantic evening of your dreams if you'll give me another chance. I'll even top it off with a dream-worthy kiss."

I stared into his soft eyes—afraid my heart was going to pop out of my chest. "Are you asking for another do-over?"

"If you prefer to call it that. Or since I understand God gives us second chances, I thought maybe you'd give me one too." His eyes twinkled, and he offered me his hand again.

I hesitated for a moment, then accepted it. *What am I doing? God would want Blake to be fully serving Him before He'd approve of a relationship between us. Wouldn't He?* We pulled back onto the road and continued our drive to Starbucks.

He pulled my hand up to his lips and kissed my fingers, sending a chill down my spine.

I gaped at him.

He moved our hands to his chest and rested them there.

I swallowed hard and turned my gaze onto the road in front of me. I should take my hand back.

But did I want to?

~

We arrived at Starbucks and placed our order. Blake handed me his phone and gave me his iTunes password. He asked me to download as many songs as I wanted. I sat at one of the taller small round tables tucked away in a corner. He joined me with our order a few songs later.

He touched my hand as I fiddled with his cell. "I do remember your kiss on my cheek. Why did you kiss me after what I'd put you through last night?"

I concentrated on his phone. "You're pretty sneaky. Acting like you're asleep. Maybe I'll try that sneaky sleep on the plane."

"Maybe I'll kiss you on the cheek." He reached over and lifted my chin. "But you didn't answer my question."

I tilted my head away from him. "You acted like a little boy. So, I tucked you in, knelt and prayed for you, and kissed your cheek."

"That 'I protect those I care about' thing." He grinned.

I looked down at his cell and added another song to his new playlist. "Blake, there's something else."

"Tell me."

"I understand your pain over Andy, but you went off with Brandi instead of finding me." I returned my focus on Blake. "Then you got drunk after I'd shared with you about my abusive aunt."

He winced and squeezed his eyes shut.

"I can't understand that, not if you care about me." I placed his phone on the table and stared at him. "It's not that you've said you care in so many words, but with the roses, and your attention this week . . ."

He held my gaze. "When Brandi asked me to join her for a drink, I thought maybe I'd loosen up enough to relax and be able to share an enjoyable evening with *you*." He picked up his coffee cup and stared at it. "I should have stopped at one."

"But you spent the entire evening with her." My voice cracked. "How did that fit into your plan to relax and share an enjoyable evening with me?"

He rubbed his hand over his face. "K, I'm sorry . . . If I could undo yesterday . . . I would." He drew his eyebrows together. "But I can't." Blake reached over and touched my hand which rested on his phone. "Hurting you was the furthest thing from my mind. Can you forgive me?"

I placed my free hand on top of his and sighed. "Yes."

I not only forgave him, but I also realized that when Blake called me K, he used my initial as an endearment and not in a belittling way as my aunt had. His nickname for me caused me to smile.

His shoulders relaxed and he gazed into my eyes. "Can we talk about us?"

My gut twisted. "Us?" I pulled my hand away from his and leaned back in my chair.

"We've talked about developing a friendship. I hope we can now. I'd like us to move past this weekend and spend time getting to know each other better."

I chuckled. "I think I know you much better today than I did Thursday morning when we started this adventure."

He shook his head. "So . . . no friendship?"

"I didn't say that or even mean to imply such a thing. I've wanted to be your friend from the beginning."

"Would you be available to join Allison, Jim, and me for dinner the first Saturday in December?"

Sounded like a family affair. Was that better or worse than a date?

"It's been a family tradition, except for the past five years."

I glanced out the window. "You want to invite me to a family tradition?"

Blake squinted. "If you don't go with me, Allison's threatened to fix me up with a blind date. I don't want that to happen."

I sighed. "You're not interested in friendship, are you?"

"Why do you say that?"

"I don't hold hands with any other friends. Also, you're inviting me to something that is considered a *family* tradition."

He frowned. "I'll tell Allison to fix me up with that

unpleasant blonde she knows."

I playfully reached over and smacked his arm. "I'd love to go as your friend. Is that doable?"

He nodded and stared out the window. I followed his gaze. A large, slender bird—smaller than a duck—ran across the parking lot. Blake stood. "A roadrunner. Let's get a better look."

I grabbed my drink, purse, and jacket and followed him outside. The dark brown and white bird, with a spiked head crest and long tail feathers, darted across the street.

I looked at Blake. "I added another item to your list of enjoyable things."

He peered deep into my eyes. "Something else should go to the top of my list."

Not me. Our friendship was moving way too fast. "Spending time with Andy? I think that should definitely be number one."

He chuckled. "Yep. My thought exactly." He helped me with my jacket and escorted me to the car. "How about lunch before we head to the airport?"

Twenty-Two

We drove north to a restaurant called Jimmy's Café. Photos of Jim's, Jimmy's, and James's covered the walls. Their menu contained many New Mexican dishes along with burgers and pizza. After we placed our order, I perused the photos. "This is quite unique."

After a short wait, our food arrived. I didn't know that *everything* you order in New Mexico includes green chili or hot and spicy seasonings. As soon as Blake saw the hot red pepper flakes on my open-faced chicken sandwich, he placed an order for sour cream.

"Thanks for taking care of me."

He picked up his fork. "Have I told you about the first time I saw you?"

Where did that come from? "The elevator?"

He shook his head. "I saw your picture on the Intranet page welcoming new employees. I thought, 'She'll be nothing but trouble.' I was right."

I frowned. "Trouble? Why would you say that?"

"I'm here with you now, taking care of you. Trouble."

I shook my head. "What was up with Debra? Every time I brought something to you from the IT Department, she'd say, 'You can go on into his office, honey. I know he'll want to say, 'Hi.' You never said, 'Hi.' You'd butcher my name and dismiss me."

The waitress brought my sour cream and asked if we needed anything else, then said she would check on us in a few minutes.

Blake's smile told me he enjoyed my jesting. After we both took a couple of bites of food, I set my fork on my plate. "I'm puzzled. You get upset with me if I allow any of the other admins to walk into your office." I squinted and leaned forward. "You made it clear from the beginning that they are to leave whatever they bring with me." I cocked my head to the right. "So, why did Debra always tell me to give departmental reports directly to you?"

"Did you see the one over there of James Dean?" Blake pointed to a photo behind me. "Ever see any of his old movies?"

I laughed. "You don't want to answer my question."

He blushed. A real red-in-the-face blush. "Debra liked you, so she sent you in. When I brought the situation to her attention, she offered to stop. She said she would ask you to leave everything with her if that's what I wanted her to do." He glanced up at the ceiling. "I told her no. I preferred that she send you in."

His comment bothered me. "So you could intimidate me?" I leaned back.

He reached over to touch my hand and looked me in the eye. "I wanted to see you. Whenever you left my office, I'd smile. Debra knew that since Cheryl's death you were the only person who put a smile on my face."

"I made you smile?" *Unbelievable.*

"Debra knows the real me." He looked around the room and repositioned himself in his chair. "She saw my attraction for you. That was her way of playing matchmaker."

"Attraction? She sent me in the first time I came to your office suite."

Blake sat back in his chair and nodded. "Yep." He took a sip of his water. "When I saw you the first time in the lobby, I knew you were at BCH for me."

I lifted my hand in front of me. "Stop. You thought I got a job there to pursue you?"

He shook his head. "I felt like God sent you there for me. I didn't want anything to do with you. Just like you didn't want to date. I felt that way too. I wasn't looking for a relationship."

The waitress refilled our water glasses and laid our bill on the table.

Blake fiddled with his napkin. "I took a risk when I requested you as my assistant. Miranda fought me big time. She wanted me to pick Rene. I knew you were the most experienced but also knew I needed to be careful."

"Careful? Because you were attracted to me but didn't want a relationship?" I frowned and bit my lower lip.

He leaned toward me and focused on my eyes. "Yes."

"That's why you were mean." I stared at the pictures on the wall behind his head. "You convinced me you hated me and wanted me gone." When I looked back at him, tiny napkin pieces laid on the table beneath his hands.

He looked down. "I'm sorry for the way I treated you."

"What changed?"

He rubbed his forehead. "When you threatened to

leave, I realized how much I needed you as my assistant and friend. I knew I had to go easier on you, because if you left, I'd miss my opportunity to prove to you that I'm a good guy. As time progressed, I . . . look." He lowered his voice. "I sense you may not be ready yet for a relationship. But I'm struggling to not think that way. I hope our friendship grows into something much more. It's better you know that up front."

I folded my hands in my lap. "Tell me about Miranda. You said she didn't want to give me the position."

He shook his head. "She used the excuse that the other internal applicants would be upset because they'd been with BCH longer. The truth is, she didn't want you to work with me."

"Why? And if she didn't want me to have the promotion, why is she so willing to give me another one?"

He leaned closer. "Where does she want to put you when you step into this new position?"

"In Bonnie's office downstairs." I touched the base of my neck. "Oh, she wants me away from you, doesn't she?"

"She's had a thing for me since she started at BCH three years ago, always trying to get me to take her to lunch or dinner or get together on the weekend." He shook his head. "I'm not interested."

"I've noticed a change in her attitude toward me the past few months. Jealousy tends to bring out the worst in all of us."

We discussed the new position a little while longer. I told him I was having second thoughts. Miranda's insistence on Alicia getting the assistant position didn't feel right.

The time came to leave for the airport. Blake paid the bill, and we strolled to the car.

I thanked him for his honesty and openness. "I understand better now why we've struggled over the past few months."

"I'll share more if you agree to have dinner with me next weekend."

I wasn't ready for a relationship. Apparently, he was. I took a deep breath. "Will you tell me whatever you told Andy?"

Blake walked me to the passenger side of his car. "I may not have a chance to talk with Allison before then. She needs to learn the truth first."

"I agree."

He opened my door for me, then climbed into the driver's side.

I looked over at him while he fastened his seatbelt. "What about this? If you want to see me next weekend, you know where I'll be on Sunday morning. We can do lunch afterward. How does that sound?"

He cleared his throat. "Sounds like a bribe."

"I didn't mean it to sound like that." I touched his arm and cocked my head.

He chuckled. "I guess attending church with you is the least I can do since I caused you to miss this morning."

We didn't talk much on our drive to the airport, which gave me time to think. If I dismissed all that happened on Saturday, I had to admit I enjoyed the trip and my time with Blake—a little too much. Where would this lead? A relationship? *Lord, help me.*

~

We boarded our plane, sat together in an exit row with only two seats, and settled in. Blake looked at his cell. "How many songs did you download?"

"Maybe twenty."

"That should keep me entertained. I hope I have my earbuds with me." He reached under the seat in front of him to grab his laptop case. He rummaged through the pocket looking for his buds.

The flight attendant approached those of us in the exit rows to verify we were capable to assist in case of an emergency. "I need a verbal yes from each of you." Blake and I were the last of those she asked. "And what about the couple on the loveseat? Are you able to assist?"

What? I stared at her.

Blake gave an immediate yes, then nudged my elbow. "Say yes."

"Yes?"

She smiled and walked down the aisle.

Blake chuckled. "That's a lovely color of red you're wearing."

I glanced down at my navy-blue jacket, squinted, and stared at him.

"Your face. Quite charming."

I shook my head. *Why did she say that?*

"Sounds official," Blake said with a chuckle, "we're a couple now."

I grabbed his arm. "Not so fast—takes two to be a couple. Let me get used to the idea of being good friends first." I released his arm and verified I'd buckled my seatbelt.

Blake found his earbuds and placed his computer case back under the seat. We were both quiet for a few minutes, then I touched his arm again. "I need to ask you something, and I need you to be honest with me."

He nodded, glanced at my hand on his arm, and smiled.

I moved my hand onto my lap. "Why did you decide to return to Nashville today and not stay here in Albuquerque with Andy for a few days?"

Blake stared down the aisle. "I wanted to make sure you and I were okay first. I didn't want you to leave when I knew you were still upset with me." He shifted in his seat and looked into my eyes. "I needed for us to talk everything through—to understand how I'd hurt you— so I could seek your forgiveness."

"You gave up time with Andy, whom you haven't seen for five years, to make sure we were okay?" I pointed at him and then back at me.

"Yes. You're that important to me."

I took a deep breath.

Blake leaned closer to my ear. "I don't want you to feel pressured if you're not ready for more than friendship. We can move as slowly . . ." He raised his eyebrows and grinned. ". . . or as quickly as you feel comfortable. I'm willing to wait."

"Thank you. That's very considerate of you."

We agreed it would be best if we didn't discuss our friendship at the office. The fewer people who knew about our time in Albuquerque, the better.

We talked about the Thanksgiving holiday, which was a few days away. He told me Jim and Allison planned to spend the day with Jim's family. Blake didn't have plans.

Without thinking it through, I invited him to join Jenny, Carl, Nicki, and me at my place. He agreed. I warned him about Nicki. "Once she warms up to you, she'll talk your ear off and say all kinds of embarrassing things."

His eyes sparkled. "I look forward to meeting her."

He offered me his hand.

I shook my head. "I'd love to hold your hand the rest of the trip home." I smirked. "I've even thought about pretending to be asleep to get a kiss on the cheek. But I need time to process everything that's happened this weekend and pray."

He leaned toward my cheek and gave me the kiss I'd asked for.

I raised my eyebrows. "I'm not sleeping."

"I don't think you plan to sleep, so I thought I'd sneak one on you while you're awake." His eyes danced. "You won't take my hand. You said you need time to pray and process. But sparks are flying everywhere." He offered me his hand again. "Sounds like I have a chance of winning you over. You need time to be sure. I can appreciate that."

I stared at his open palm, slid my hand into his, and gave it a gentle squeeze. Then I sat back in my seat and closed my eyes.

This can't be good. He's already won my heart.

A Note from LuAnn

Dear Reader,

Thank you for reading *Only a Glimpse*. If you enjoyed Blake and Keedryn's story, please post a review on Amazon.

I hope you'll join me for Book 2 in the *Love Comes Again* series—*Let Him Go*.

A story of love, acceptance, and forgiveness, *Let Him Go* continues Blake and Keedryn's romance. Thanksgiving dinner brings Blake and Keedryn's family together. A week later, Keedryn and Blake join Allison and her husband for what turns out to be a romantic dinner despite family members present. After a perfect evening, Keedryn suffers from a crushed heart, and trouble brews at the office. A new policy goes into effect that disrupts and could destroy Blake and Keedryn's newfound love. To make matters worse, Wes steps in and tries to win Keedryn's heart, and Blake's wife's former friend makes a move on Blake. Can Keedryn's family convince her that Blake is worth fighting for? Will Blake forgive himself and God for his wife's death and realize the blessings God has placed before him?

To be notified when future books are released, including, *Let Him Go*, please sign up for my blog and e-newsletter at www.luannkedwards.com.

Let's connect through my website's contact page at https://www.luannkedwards.com/take-action, Facebook https://www.facebook.com/luannkedwards, or Twitter https://twitter.com/LuAnnKEdwards1. I'd love to hear from you.

Thank you, and God bless!

LuAnn

Acknowledgements

First, I'd like to thank my Lord and Savior. You placed the desire in me many years ago to write. Although it has taken me a long time, I am grateful You didn't give up on me, and I thank You for the lovely story of hope you birthed within my heart.

To my husband Kenn—you are the better half. Thank you for your love, support, and the reassurance to keep writing.

Gerry Wakeland, thank you for asking me to write for the church blog and for the push to attend my first writers conference several years ago.

I am thankful for my critique group and first readers who shared great ideas and offered their support and encouragement along the way. Thank you, Wendy, Marylin, Glenda, Gerry, Moss, Kim, Leah, Kiran, Julie, and Courtney. And to my fellow Bible study gals who haven't already been named—Pam, Kathi, Kelly, and Erica—I appreciate each one of you.

Thank you, Larry J. Leech II for your thorough critique and assistance and Lee Warren as the story's final pair of eyes before I sent it to the publisher.

Finally, I would like to thank Winged Publications for the opportunity to publish my debut novel and series.